Avoiding the Merry Viscount

Romancing the Ton, Book 1

Christina Diane

ARE YOU SIGNED UP FOR DRAGONBLADE'S BLOG?

You'll get the latest news and information on exclusive giveaways, exclusive excerpts, coming releases, sales, free books, cover reveals and more.

Check out our complete list of authors, too!

No spam, no junk. That's a promise!

Sign Up Here

www.dragonbladepublishing.com

Dearest Reader;

Thank you for your support of a small press. At Dragonblade Publishing, we strive to bring you the highest quality Historical Romance from some of the best authors in the business. Without your support, there is no 'us', so we sincerely hope you adore these stories and find some new favorite authors along the way.

Happy Reading!

CEO, Dragonblade Publishing

Additional Dragonblade books by Author Christina Diane

Romancing the Ton Series
Avoiding the Merry Viscount (Book 1)

Dragonblade Anthologies
Dukes All Night Long

PROLOGUE

Elias

Sussex, England
December 1799

E LIAS ARMSTRONG, THE young Viscount Snowdon, stuffed a few more things into his pack, and motioned for his three closest friends to follow him downstairs. The boys were all on break from school and spending a couple of weeks at Elias's home before the holidays to partake in hunting, snowball fights, and whatever else four boys the age of four-and-ten might get up to during the wintertime in the country.

The boys each held their hunting rifles and their packs, which they had stuffed with food and a change of clothing. They made their way to the drawing room in search of Elias's parents.

Unfortunately for them, they found Diana and Hannah, Elias's and Hudson's younger sisters.

"We want to come too," Elias's sister, Diana, whined.

His best friend Hudson had brought his younger sister Hannah with him for the visit since Diana and Hannah were also the best of friends. Elias's and Hudson's parents were close, so the children had all practically grown up together.

Elias had hoped that having Hannah in attendance would keep his sister occupied so she wouldn't try to follow them, but instead it gave them two young girls to argue with. He was thankful that his other sisters were too young to team up with the pair. Diana and Hannah were both the age of six, and just old enough to follow them about.

"You are not coming with us, sister," he replied. "And that is final." The boys would stay overnight in one of the hunting cabins at the far edge of their estate. There were a few on their property, but they chose the one farthest from the house to feel more like they were getting away from everyone. And the adventure would be far less enjoyable if they had to keep an eye on the two little girls.

Diana clasped her arms across her chest and harrumphed. "You don't get to decide that."

"But I do." Their father, the Earl of Snowdon, crept up behind Diana and scooped her into his arms. "Let the boys have their fun, while you and Hannah have the run of the house without them pestering you."

Elias's father nodded to him where Diana couldn't see. He had always been close to his father, as the firstborn and the only son of the earl's four children.

"Come here, dearest," their mother told Diana, coming to stand beside their father. "We shall have a fun time without the boys. I shall let you and Hannah try on some of my jewelry, and we'll have tea this afternoon with just us ladies. What would you both think about that?"

The girls started dancing about and each clasped one of his mother's hands.

"Will you also take us for a ride?" Diana asked. "I wish to learn to ride a horse like you do, Mama."

"Your papa and I agreed you could start lessons in the spring," their mama replied. Their mother loved her horse almost as much as she loved her husband and children. She wasn't one to sit inside the entire day, as she needed time each day to get out and ride. "Let's be off and tell Cook about our special tea."

Elias's mother gave him one last glance. "Have a fun time, my sweet boy," she said, using the pet name she'd called him for as long as he could remember, even though he was ever nearing manhood. She flashed him a grin and then led the girls, bouncing, out of the room.

"You boys will be careful and behave yourselves, will you not?" the earl asked as soon as the females had departed the room.

"Of course, Papa," Elias replied. "We shall return tomorrow afternoon in time for tea."

His father laughed. "I don't doubt it. There is no way the four of you have enough food in those packs to allay your hunger for any longer than that."

Elias believed his father had a point. "Have Cook make extra tarts and biscuits. We are sure to eat them all."

"I am certain your mother has already done so. She has a knack for being on top of these things."

The love that shone in his father's eyes was evident. His parents were a love match, a rarity in their society. They didn't last long in each other's presence without succumbing to their deep affection. Part of him found their displays embarrassing in front of his friends, but Elias also secretly smiled to himself, knowing that his parents' love for each other was so strong.

He wouldn't admit it to the boys, but he hoped that one day he might find a marriage like theirs. Not anytime soon, of course. But when the time came, he wanted to experience the deep, true love his parents had.

"Are we ready to be off, then?" Jude asked, nodding toward the door.

"Yes, let us depart," Elias said. "See you tomorrow, Papa."

Elias, Jude, Hudson, and Matt each donned their greatcoats and then departed toward the stables. Their horses were readied, and once they had each mounted and secured their unloaded rifles in their laps, they took off for the hunting cabin. They wanted to get out of the house and enjoy a bit of adventure on their own, but if they were lucky enough to shoot a stag for their troubles, all the better.

Riding across the snowy fields and through the forests of trees to get to the hunting cabin took every bit of a half an hour for them to get there. The cabin had a small stable area where the horses would sleep for the night, and they each donned a blanket which should keep them warm.

The boys settled and secured their horses and then entered the cabin. Elias and the others cheered when they found the cabin had been equipped with a bunch of firewood, more blankets, and extra food. His mother had coordinated it all for them, no doubt. She didn't miss a thing.

Dropping their bags to the floor and placing their guns on the rack mounted by the door, Jude and Hudson plopped into chairs while Matt and Elias set to work on starting the fire.

"Will we get to help collect some of the greenery for the Christmas Eve decorations?" Jude asked.

Matt stacked the wood in the fireplace, then Elias lit it. He stoked the fire to get it to the point of high flames that emitted a warm heat.

"If you want to. Haven't you done so before?" Elias asked.

"No," Jude answered, frowning.

Jude's mother had died giving birth to him, and the group of friends knew very little about his father, the Marquess Sandon, since they'd never met him.

"Let's all help then." Matt sat on the floor in front of the settee and leaned back against it. "It would be great fun. We can let the girls help us, and that should keep them from saying we did nothing with them all break."

Matt was one of the most jovial people that one would ever meet. And the most dependable and helpful of their group. His father was the Earl of Wilton, and Elias knew Matt would be an admirable peer of the realm when he inherited the title.

Hudson groaned. "Do we have to? That sounds dreadful."

He had been Elias's closest friend for years, given that they had practically shared a cradle. Hudson's and Hannah's parents would arrive in two days to spend the holidays with the lot of them. Hudson was a good friend, but he wasn't always the friendliest sort. It's a shame his father wasn't a duke, because he'd have the broody, haughty duke persona down cold. But alas, his father was an earl, just as Elias's. Hudson's father was the Earl of Onslow.

"Come now, Hud," Elias said. "Matt is right. It won't kill us to do something with the girls. It is Christmas after all. We can consider it our gift to them."

"Fine. As long as there aren't any of those kissing balls anywhere," Hudson replied, crossing his arms.

"I don't believe so." Elias shrugged one of his shoulders before plopping onto the settee. "It will not be a big party. Lord and Lady Onslow are the only ones coming besides us. Our parents don't need a kissing ball as an excuse to kiss in front of us all."

Hudson wrinkled his nose. His parents were also a love match, and he suffered the same affectionate displays in his home that Elias had.

"Speaking of kissing," Jude began, changing the subject. "I think that Sarah, the daughter of Mister Pembroke, is sweet on Matt."

Matt waved him off. "Not me. I'm just kind to her. She has eyes for Elias. At least I should hope so after what I walked in on." Then he stared knowingly at Elias.

"All right, all right. I kissed her. Only once." She was their professor's daughter and visited the school every so often. He was almost certain she was a year or so older than him.

Elias glanced around the room and saw his friends all staring at him as if they expected him to say more about the matter.

"What? It was just a quick kiss. She said she thought I was handsome, and that was that."

Jude smirked at him. "And where were your hands?"

"At my sides," Elias said. Although, if he could go back, he might have been a bit more strategic about the placement.

"And what if I hadn't walked in on you?" Matt asked.

Elias shrugged. "I guess we'll never know." He wasn't certain what else could occur beyond kissing but could tell with his eyes that a girl's body differed from a boy's. But he wouldn't admit his lack of knowledge to his friends.

"Now that we know Elias has kissed her, he's ruined her for the rest of us." Jude feigned irritation before grinning at him.

The boys all laughed, and Elias rolled his eyes at all of them. It hadn't been a big deal. He had just wondered what it would be like to kiss a girl, and the opportunity presented itself. But he supposed they were of the age to experiment and learn of such things.

Elias always confided everything in his father, and when he told his father about his kiss, it was just before his friends were set to arrive. His father said he wanted to have a talk with him about what occurred between men and women after the holidays and everyone had returned home. It only made him all the more curious.

"Let's dig into some of the food that Lady Snowdon must have sent." Hudson rose from his chair.

They descended on the basket of food like locusts, eating their fill for their dinner, laughing and bantering with each other as they did so. The boys retold some of their favorite stories from school and about the mischievous times they had.

Elias sent a silent thought of gratitude to his mother for sending the extra food, because what she sent was completely gone and they'd need the food they had in their packs to break their fast in the morning.

It had grown dark. Each of the boys grabbed a blanket and settled into a spot by the roaring fire that Jude had tended.

Hudson surprised all of them by telling them a ghost story that was set at Christmas. He wasn't known for storytelling or creativity, but it was an interesting story that had them all leaning closer with their blankets right until the very end.

After a few more stories, they all fell asleep, each of them sprawled out around the furniture in the room. One or two of them could have taken the bed within the single bed chamber in the cabin, but they had all opted to camp out together in the main room.

The next morning, Hudson woke them all up so they could try for a morning hunt. Once they had donned their greatcoats and bundled themselves in their warm coverings, they traversed the woods as quietly as they could, settling into a spot where they could observe the area from behind several large stones.

There was packed snow on the ground, but it wasn't actively snowing. It was a little late in the season to hunt, but they hoped that luck might be on their side.

An hour or so later, that wouldn't appear to be the case. They had sat in silence, patiently waiting, but the snow began to fall, and only fell harder as the wind picked up. They hadn't seen a single animal out and about. Deciding they would freeze to death if they remained outside for much longer, they gave up and made their way back to the cabin.

Elias revived the fire while the rest of his friends peeled off their coverings so they could dry before the fire. They would warm up at the cabin for a few more hours and hope the snow stopped before they made the ride back to the main house.

Conversation filled the room as the boys spoke of the upcoming holiday and the treats they couldn't wait to partake in on Christmas Eve and Christmas Day. They devoured all the food from their packs. After a few hours, the snow had stopped, and they decided it was time to make the ride back to Elias's house.

They dressed in their coats and warm coverings again. Elias separated the logs so that the fire would die out in the fireplace, while they each packed all of their things into their satchels. All the boys ventured to the stables and mounted their horses to set off.

The wind was harsh against their cheeks, but otherwise it was a pleasant ride. They trotted into the stables and leapt from their horses.

"My lord," one groom started, his eyes cast to his feet. "Your father asked to have you attend him directly upon your return. We were just about to send someone to fetch you."

"Is something amiss?" Elias asked.

The man met his gaze, and sadness marred his expression. "It's not my place, my lord. You must speak with his lordship."

Elias dropped his pack to the ground before addressing his friends. "Tend to things here and meet me in the drawing room. I must go to my father."

Hudson nodded and took Elias's gun from his hand. Elias sprinted toward the house. A footman was just inside the door.

"Where is my father?" Elias asked, his tone harsher than usual.

The footman wore the same somber expression the groom had. "I believe he's with her ladyship. In her chamber."

His words made little sense. Elias's parents always slept in the same bed. His mother never used the chamber that was designated for the countess. He must mean the chamber his parents shared.

Elias took off again down the corridor from the back of the house until it opened up to the foyer that led to the grand staircase. He climbed the stairs two at a time, barreling to his parents' chamber. Not bothering to knock, he threw the door open, and the chamber was empty. What was going on? Where was his father and why did he wish to see him?

Continuing farther down the hall to a chamber he couldn't remember the last time he'd visited, other than perhaps when Diana roped him into a game of hide-and-seek, he approached the closed door. Something nagged at him, and he opened the door more cautiously this time, poking his head inside.

Nothing could have prepared him for what he saw. His mother laid on the bed, having suffered some kind of accident given the amount of bloody bandages. One leg and arm were obviously broken and had been wrapped in dressings, but the blood seeped through the white cloth wrapping. There was blood around her midsection, and her head was wrapped with another bloody cloth.

"Papa?" he called, his voice barely above a whisper. He wasn't even sure it was his own voice as he took in the shocking scene before him.

"Come in and close the door," his father commanded. His papa, the man he loved and respected most in the world, and looked up to for all things, was a mixture of fury, pain, and sadness.

His papa held his mama's hand while a doctor continued working with a grim expression. Elias drew a deep breath, his entire thin body trembling from the sight before him. Somehow he found the ability to step closer to the bed, coming to stand by his father to stay out of the way of the doctor who worked from the other side of the bed.

Elias remained quiet and fisted his hands at his sides, digging his fingernails into his palms to give himself something to focus on so he wouldn't break into sobs beside his father, who appeared only moments away from slipping into a state of madness.

The doctor finally looked up from where he worked and caught his father's gaze, shaking his head and his expression somber. "I'm very sorry, my lords. Her injuries are too severe. She won't survive. I have given her laudanum to make her comfortable, but I don't expect her to live much longer."

"No!" his father cried out. "No. Emily, please. Don't leave me. You can't leave me." His father was falling apart before his eyes, sobbing and holding his mother's hand to his face. "No…no…no…You can't. I can't live without you." Each of his words came out in between sobs.

Tears streamed down Elias's cheeks as he clenched his fists harder, trying to maintain some level of composure for his father's benefit. He glanced at his mother, who appeared as if she were sleeping peacefully, which was in stark contrast to the pale, almost blue tone of her skin and the devastating appearance of her injuries. Elias glanced away, meeting the eye of the doctor, who cast him a sympathetic expression.

"What happened?" Elias asked the doctor.

"She suffered an accident while riding. I am told that her horse returned to the stables without her and your father and grooms went out looking for her and found her like this in the snow."

His father sobbed again and laid across his wife. "Take me. Please don't leave me, Emily," his father pleaded, as if there was someone listening to him. His shoulders shook and his chest heaved.

Elias had never seen his father in such a state, and it was more than he could bear. Elias was devastated knowing that he'd lose his mother, and scared that he might lose his father too.

Drawing a deep breath, Elias wiped the tears from his eyes. "Papa," he whispered.

Suddenly, his father shot up. "No. Please, no. She's not breathing. Help her."

The doctor put his fingers to her neck, and his shoulders slumped after a few moments. "I'm sorry, my lord. She is gone."

✦》》✕《《✦

ON CHRISTMAS EVE, two days later, Elias did his best to help his sisters gather the greenery to decorate for Christmas. It felt wrong and sad to do so without their mother, but Lady Onslow convinced him it would help the girls take their minds off of things. The Onslows had insisted on staying and helping the family through the devastating time, and Elias appreciated them beyond what words could convey.

Lady Onslow cradled his youngest sister Grace in her arms and watched while Matt, Hudson, and Jude carried baskets and helped Diana and Hannah cut the greenery they wanted. Elias carried Jenny, his three-year-old sister, since she wanted to help too.

He was thankful Jenny and Grace were too young to understand the gravity of the situation. Diana was devastated, but having Hannah and Lady Onslow there had been a tremendous help.

Their father hadn't left his bedchamber since it happened. He would only allow Elias and Lord Onslow in, as he didn't want to frighten the girls. Lord Onslow tried to convince Elias's father to join the family, that it would make him feel better to be around his children, but his father just hugged his pillow and cried.

Elias would have never believed it was possible for the man he'd always viewed as the strongest and most level-headed person there was to crumble beneath the weight of his pain.

"Are you all right?" Hudson asked, appearing beside him.

"That one, brother," Jenny called, pointing to the branch she wanted. Her little nose and cheeks were red from the cold, but at least her eyes were dry. His heart panged at the realization that his sisters wouldn't have a mother to teach them about becoming young ladies and running a household with the efficiency their mother had. That job would fall to governesses and tutors.

Elias closed his eyes, fighting the emotion within him, trying to harden it into a tight ball and swallow it down. "Will you cut that for her?" he asked, ignoring Hudson's question.

Hudson did as he asked and placed the branch in the basket that Elias held in his free hand.

They walked in silence to join the others, since everyone's baskets had been filled. Once everyone was inside, Lady Onslow ordered tea and warm milk. Another task that his mother should be there to do. She would have had the most elaborate spread with all of their favorite treats.

Elias set Jenny down and she ran to Lady Onslow and crawled up to sit beside her on the settee, where Hudson's mama held a sleeping Grace. Diana and Hannah sat together in the chair next to her, and Hannah held Diana's hand while they waited. Lord Onslow sat in the chair on the other side of the settee, watching his wife with the girls.

Elias moved to stand before the fire, putting his back to everyone in the room. He wasn't alone for long before all three of his friends had joined his side. Hudson on his left, then Jude on his right, with Matt on the other side of Jude. They said nothing, but just stared into the fire with him. He found their presence comforting, and the fact that they didn't speak even more so.

After a quarter hour of standing before the fire, Elias finally spoke. "Thank you for being here."

"We will be wherever you need us to be." Hudson clasped his shoulder.

"Can you keep an eye on my sisters in case Lady Onslow should require help? I wish to visit Papa."

His friends all nodded and moved back to the other side of the room, where tea was being brought in on a cart.

Elias made his way upstairs and to the room that his parents had shared for his entire life. When he opened the door, his father was sitting in a chair by the window. At least he was out of bed, which made Elias feel hopeful his father might at least be making a bit of progress.

"Papa?"

"My son," he quavered.

Elias moved across the room and stood near the window that his father looked out. He remained silent, unsure what to say to make things better for his father. He was aware how deeply his father and mother had loved each other, but to see that love ripped apart and his father's heart shattered and irreparable made him rethink everything he thought about love.

"How are the girls?" his father asked.

"They miss you," he answered honestly.

His father closed his eyes and drew a deep breath. "I miss them too." He paused for a few moments, then spoke again. "They all look so much like her. Especially Diana, who also has her mother's spirit. I just...I don't know if I can."

Diana looked like a miniature version of their mother. Although each of his mother's children inherited her deep blue eyes. And each of the girls had her blonde hair, while Elias looked more like his father with darker hair, except for the blue eyes.

"They need you. I'm doing the best I can. But I'm not enough," Elias choked.

"I know, son," his father said, running his hand down his face. "I ask too much of you. But I don't know how to live in a world where your mother doesn't. I know I must find a way to carry on for you and your sisters." His father closed his eyes and wiped his cheeks again. "Have a bath sent up for me. I will join you for Christmas Eve dinner after I have bathed and dressed."

His father was true to his word and emerged from his bed-chamber looking every bit the aristocratic earl, even if his red, puffy eyes told of his pain. Diana and Jenny ran to him and hugged his legs when he appeared, and to Elias's surprise, his father's eyes welled, but he kept any tears from falling.

They had a somewhat quiet dinner. Conversation was painful and awkward, but they all did their best to carry on. It wasn't conventional or fashionable, but Lady Onslow continued to hold Grace throughout dinner, while Jenny sat in a chair beside her. She said it didn't seem right to send the girls away to the nursery on Christmas Eve. Elias knew if his mother were there, she wouldn't have sent them away either.

Once she finished eating, Jenny jumped down from her chair and ran to their father, who picked her up and put her in his lap. It didn't go unnoticed by Elias that his father left his meal untouched, and he knew he'd need to ensure his father remedied his lack of appetite soon. He was almost certain the man hadn't eaten a single bite of food since they'd lost her.

After dinner, they all moved to the drawing room. Lady Onslow played the pianoforte and led the group in a couple of carols. Elias watched the expressions of his sisters and was glad that, for even a moment, they experienced a bit of joy to overcome the sadness that awaited them in the days ahead.

Papa hobbled away from the group to stand by the fire, staring at the candle that was lit on the mantle. They had lit it in memory of Elias's mother, so a part of her might be with them that evening.

She would have made Christmas morning a grand affair, always giving each of them a special gift with a handwritten note.

Not that Elias would ever admit it to anyone, but the note from his mother had always been his favorite gift every year. And his heart broke all over again at the realization that he'd never receive one from her again.

Before he became emotional in front of the entire room, Elias moved to stand next to his father, their shoulders almost touching. Elias clasped his hands behind his back, drawing a deep breath as he stared into the fire, attempting to push aside all of his pain to be strong for his father and sisters.

Out of the corner of his eye, he saw his father's head turn, so he turned his to meet his father's gaze. The pain and misery in his father's eyes from the unimaginable loss shone through, heavier than it had in the last couple of days. At that moment, witnessing the grief that threatened to crush his father beneath it, Elias knew. He'd never allow himself to fall in love. Love would hold no place in his future.

CHAPTER ONE

Lydia

London, England
April 1811
12 years later

MISS LYDIA CARY, only daughter of Viscount Cary, pressed herself against the brick wall at the corner of Berkeley Square, her pulse racing frantically. The late afternoon sun hung low in the gray London sky, casting long shadows between the elegant townhouses and providing perfect cover for what she had planned.

I am quite mad, she decided. A well-bred young lady simply did not sneak from her family's townhouse to visit a gentleman unchaperoned. But then again, a well-bred young lady probably didn't burn with the same restless curiosity that had plagued Lydia for days.

It was Clint's fault, really. Her cheeks heated at the use of his given name, even if it wasn't the most scandalous impropriety she'd experienced with the man. He'd been so charming during their quiet courtship, so different from the other stuffy gentlemen who'd paid court to her. But he'd always been a charmer. His family's estate was located near hers, so their families had known each other for as long as she could remember.

He'd always been flirtatious toward her, but then everything had changed when she'd become of marrying age. Lydia appreciated how he didn't make a big show of courting her, instead doting his charms on her, whispering intimate words of desire and longing. It stirred things in her that were wanton to say the least.

She had every intention of marrying the man, and he was hardly a stranger, so surely she could be forgiven for allowing his hands between her thighs. And that she had also learned what lay in wait between his. Clint had tempted and teased her, introducing her to an intense pleasure that she'd never known was possible. He told her it was only a taste of what awaited them.

After that encounter, where she could no longer claim that her hands were innocent, she informed her father that she would only marry Clint.

And regardless of what kind of wanton it made her, all she could think about was the pleasure that Clint had given her. She longed to explore the sensations further, to understand what it meant to desire and experience her future husband so completely. And with their betrothal announcement approaching soon, surely it hardly mattered if she waited until their wedding night to be with him in that way.

At least, that's what she'd told herself when she'd slipped from her family's townhouse three streets away, claiming a sudden headache that required her to rest in her chamber. Her maid, Tilly, was visiting her sister for the afternoon, and her parents were receiving callers in the front parlor—she could hear the Duchess of Marlborough's distinctive laugh echoing through the halls. The timing was perfect.

Lydia straightened her bonnet and smoothed her skirts, though her hands were unsteady. Clint's townhouse loomed just across the square, its imposing façade both welcoming and intimidating. She had never visited his London home, as that would be entirely improper. But she would surprise him and show him how much she wanted the things that he promised.

Drawing a breath that did little to calm her nerves, she crossed the square with quick, determined steps, resolved in what she'd set out to do.

Rather than approach the front entrance where she would surely be seen and announced, Lydia made her way to the side of the house, and located the servants' entrance. Her heart hammered in her chest as she tested the door handle, finding it unlocked, just as she expected.

She slipped inside what appeared to be a narrow corridor leading from the kitchen quarters. The scent of roasting meat and fresh bread reached her and made her regret that she'd skipped luncheon. Her stomach had been in knots as she'd worked out her plans, and she couldn't get herself to sit still long enough to eat a single bite.

Moving as quietly as she could, Lydia made her way through the servants' passages, hoping to find stairs that would lead to where Clint's study would likely be located. It couldn't be too difficult to find, since most townhouses followed a similar layout.

Then she realized that she hadn't considered what she would do if he weren't home. Wait for him? She supposed that was all she could do. It would be devastating to have come so far only to leave feeling silly and unsatisfied. But she would press on and decide what to do if she must. With any luck, he'd be where she hoped to find him, and that would be that.

After what felt like an eternity of navigating the corridors, she found a narrow staircase and climbed carefully, listening for any sounds that might indicate approaching servants. At the top, she discovered a door that opened into what was clearly the main part of the house.

The house felt oddly quiet, almost hushed. Despite Lydia's attempts at stealth, her footsteps echoed more loudly than usual. She moved down the corridor, checking each room she passed until she found what could only be Clint's study. There was a heavy oak door and masculine furnishings visible through the gap.

As she approached, she could hear voices from within—his familiar baritone and what sounded like a female voice, though she couldn't make out the words through the heavy oak door that stood slightly ajar. Perhaps his housekeeper was attending to some matter. She would wait until the woman departed.

But as she drew closer, the voices became clearer, and what she heard made her blood turn to ice.

"That's it," Clint's voice, thick and breathless in a way she'd never heard before, though there was something familiar about the tone that made her stomach clench. "Just like that. You know exactly what I like."

A woman's voice responded with what could only be described as a moan of pleasure, followed by wet, rhythmic sounds that Lydia's innocent mind struggled to identify even as her traitorous body somehow understood their meaning.

Her heart froze in her chest and tears welled in the corners of her eyes. Surely she was mistaken. Surely the man she'd known for years who had told her how much he wished to marry her, and to be with her forever, he would never—

"Much better than that inexperienced little mouse I'm to marry," Clint continued, his voice rough with pleasure. "You know how to use that mouth for its proper purpose."

The words hit Lydia like a physical blow. Her hands flew to her mouth to stifle her gasp, but she couldn't leave without facing him. Her shaking fingers pressed against the door, pushing it open just enough for her to see inside.

What she witnessed would burn itself into her mind for years to come. Clint stood behind his desk, his breeches unfastened and pushed down, his head thrown back in obvious pleasure. Before him, on her knees on the expensive Persian carpet, was a pretty young blonde maid.

The girl's head moved rhythmically, and the sounds they were making left no doubt as to what was occurring. Lydia's limited understanding of such matters suddenly became horrifyingly clear.

"But don't worry, kitten. I may need the innocent chit's dowry, but I'll still put this mouth of yours—and more—to work regularly."

Clint's words destroyed Lydia's heart completely. She released a small cry, unable to stop herself.

At that moment, the maid's eyes opened, seeing Lydia through the crack in the door. Terror filled the young woman's gaze, and she tried to pull away, but Clint's hands tightened in her hair.

"Don't you dare stop!" he snarled, and then his gaze followed the maid's to the door. When his eyes met Lydia's, instead of showing shame or surprise, a slow, cruel smile spread across his face.

"Well, well," he purred, never loosening his grip on the maid as he rocked himself into her mouth. "Look who's decided to pay an improper visit. How delightfully scandalous of you, my dear. Perhaps you will prove to be a bit more lively than I thought."

Lydia's vision blurred as tears of rage and humiliation filled her eyes. She stumbled backward from the door, her whole body shaking as her supposed betrothed continued to take his pleasure from another woman right in front of her.

"Don't run away now, sweet Lydia. This is your education. Best you learn what men require." His breathing grew more labored, speaking in short bursts as his hips increased in speed. "And accept that I'll always need more than you. I shall employ women in our home who please me, so you might as well become friendly with them. Because warming your bed shall never keep me satisfied."

Lydia should have punched him square in the nose, or clawed at his lying face. She should have told him what a vile bastard he was. But instead, her body had a mind of its own and she turned and ran away from the scene.

Her feet carried her through the corridors without conscious thought, back through the maze of passages until she found the servants' entrance. She burst through the door and into the street, running until her stays cut into her ribs and her lungs burned, finally stopping several blocks away to press herself against a lamppost as great, heaving sobs wracked her body.

How could she have been so foolish? How could she have believed his pretty words, his tender touches, meant anything beyond his desire to secure her dowry? That's all she was to him—a sum in a ledger book.

And one of many women's bodies to use. How many others had there been? How many would there be once Lydia became his wife?

The memory of his satisfied smile as he watched her discover his true nature made her stomach turn. He had taken pleasure in her shock and pain, and demonstrated exactly how little he thought of her.

This was the man she'd intended to marry. The man she'd considered allowing greater intimacies. The man she'd believed herself to… love? She had never thought herself to be in love with him.

And she realized what a fool she had been. She had been so caught up in his words and the intensity of the climax she felt that it had overtaken all of her good sense. She knew better, and she had allowed herself to fall into the trap of a handsome man with a wicked hand, and mistaken the whole matter for some kind of deeper affection. Affection that, if she'd thought with her head instead of the place between her thighs, she'd have already known wasn't love.

His plot would have worked if she hadn't discovered his true nature. Lydia would have been trapped at his side forever. So perhaps she owed a debt of gratitude to the maid on her knees with Clint's cock in her mouth.

Lydia wiped her eyes and continued back toward her home.

By the time she reached her family's townhouse, she had composed herself enough to slip inside through the servants' entrance. She reentered the main corridor and listened for the indication that her parents still had guests. There was no way that she could face anyone else. It would be impossible enough to face her father and find a way to explain to him why he must call off the betrothal.

She continued through the house and found her father in his study, reviewing correspondence, her mother seated nearby with her embroidery.

"Papa?" Lydia's voice came out smaller than she intended. "Mama? Might I speak with you both? It's… it's rather urgent."

Her parents looked up with immediate concern. Her mother set aside her needlework while her father gestured to a chair.

"Of course, dearest. Come, sit." Her mother's gentle face showed worry. "How are you feeling? Your headache?"

Lydia twisted her hands together, noting how they still shook. "Papa, I… I have something of great importance to discuss with you. With both of you."

Her father studied her face, and she knew he could see her distress despite her attempts to hide it. He had always been protective of her and she was unsure what he would do once he learned what Clint had done. And what she had done.

"What troubles you, my dear?"

"I cannot marry Lord Durham." The words tumbled out in a rush. "I will not marry him. I know we've discussed the match, and I know he's expressed his intentions, but I will not become his wife."

Her father's eyebrows rose. Legally, he was the one who would decide if she would marry Clint, but he had always said the choice would be hers. "Indeed? This is rather sudden, particularly given your enthusiasm for the gentleman only yesterday. Has something occurred?"

Lydia's cheeks burned with shame. "I… I discovered something about his character that makes him entirely unsuitable as a husband."

"What sort of discovery?" Her father's voice had taken on a sharper edge.

There was nothing for it but the truth. "I went to his townhouse this afternoon." At her mother's sharp intake of breath, Lydia hurried on. "I know I should not have gone alone, but I wished to speak with him privately about our future. Instead, I found him... engaged in certain activities with one of his maids. And I beg you to not make me speak further about what I saw."

That was the least she could hope for. That she didn't have to describe the scene in detail to her father. She had already been embarrassed enough to last a lifetime.

The quiet that stretched between them was unbearable. Her father's face darkened like a thundercloud.

"You went to his home alone?" His voice was dangerously low.

"Yes, Papa, but—"

"Do you have any idea what could have happened? What scandal you risked?" Lord Cary rose from his chair, his face flushed with anger. "Lydia, I am appalled by your lack of judgment! A young lady does not call upon a gentleman unchaperoned. Ever!"

"But Papa, what I discovered—"

"Is exactly the sort of information you never should have been in a position to discover!" He began pacing, his hands clenched behind his back. "The fact that you witnessed his... indiscretions... only proves how dangerous your actions were. What if he had not been occupied? What if he had taken liberties? What if someone had seen you enter or leave?"

Lydia's eyes filled with tears. "I'm sorry, Papa. Truly. But the most pressing matter is that I can't marry him. Please don't make me."

"That bastard is worse than a blackguard," her father barked. "He's a libertine monster. I'll not see my daughter wed to such a man, no matter what arrangements have been discussed."

Lydia released a long, relieved sigh. "Thank you, Papa."

"However," he continued, his tone becoming stern again, "we must ensure that your reputation remains intact. Fortunately, no betrothal has been formally announced, and very few knew of his interest. I'll handle the matter quietly and make it clear to the scoundrel that he is to never speak to you again. As far as society is concerned, there was never, and never will be, any understanding between our families."

Lady Cary moved to place a comforting hand on Lydia's shoulder. "Your father is right, dearest. And this must never be spoken of again. The scandal would destroy you, and that monster would escape all consequences."

"I understand." Lydia wiped her eyes. "And Papa? I'm truly sorry for my conduct today. It was reckless and foolish."

"Indeed it was." His voice gentled slightly. "But you're safe, and you've learned something valuable about his character before it was too late."

"What if I never wish to marry now, Papa?"

Her father rose from his chair and moved around the desk, pulling Lydia to her feet. He embraced her in a comforting hug, and the quiet sobs left her body in the safety of her father's arms.

"My dear girl," he whispered. "Not all men are like that bastard. We shall take greater care to ensure you aren't fooled by a disreputable rake again."

Lydia nodded into her father's shoulder and regained control of herself. Pulling back, she gave her father a small nod. "Thank you for understanding, Papa."

"Anything for our dearest girl. Now go and rest after the trying events of the day while I tend to this matter."

As Lydia left her father's study, she questioned how she would find what she now knew she required in a husband. They would have to prove his fidelity beyond doubt. She would not—could not—live with the knowledge that the man she'd married thought so little of her that he'd betray their vows.

She'd been willing to give Clint everything, and he'd seen her as nothing more than a convenient purse with legs. The pretty words and tender touches meant nothing if they came from a man who saw women as objects for his use rather than people deserving of respect and loyalty.

Lydia Cary would marry for love and faithfulness, or she would not marry at all. And she would never again trust a damn rake.

CHAPTER TWO

Elias

December 1811

ELIAS ROLLED HIS eyes when the sounds of carolers reached his ears as his carriage rolled down the cold streets of London. Fortunately, the sound was gone as quickly as it approached once the carriage turned on another street heading out of town. He wasn't certain how he felt about the events that awaited him at his country home over Christmas.

Not that he hated the holiday, exactly. But what he hated was the pain in his father's eyes and the hole left in their family after his mother passed, which felt far wider around the anniversary of her passing. He frequently recalled that first Christmas without her, when his father used every ounce of his strength to pretend for the benefit of Elias's younger sisters.

It has been twelve years, and time has made none of them miss her any less. The tears were fewer, and his father had gone on to ensure their estates thrived and that each of his children were loved, but the hole remained.

"Surely attending Diana's house party won't be all that bad," Jude said from his seat in the carriage, facing Elias.

"You are telling me you are looking forward to being trapped for a sennight with whatever eager young chits my sister has invited?" Elias asked, not bothering to hide his irritation. Diana had requested him to arrive a day before the others to help with the remaining preparations and to greet each of the guests as they arrived. He and Jude had decided to travel together, sending their valets ahead of them to prepare for their arrival.

He knew Diana hoped to fill the hole in their lives with a house full of people, and it only made Elias dread the holiday more.

"Not at all, but I'm certain we will have a grand time. You will play the part of the merry viscount and dodge all the marriage-minded ladies. And I shall support you in such an endeavor," Jude said, raising his arms and clasping his fingers behind his head as he leaned into the squabs.

Jude, who had officially become Marquess Sandon, was the most notorious rake of the *ton*. Elias might have been on his way to earning that title for himself if he didn't also have sisters to help marry well. He attempted to conceal his libertine lifestyle somewhat more than his friend did.

Diana had made her come out last season, and it was his job to ensure that she didn't take up with the wrong sort of gentleman, which he enlisted the help of Jude, Hudson, and Matt to do.

Seeing to Diana's prospects should have been a role that his father tended to, but Papa didn't wish to leave the country. He preferred to be where he felt closest to Mama and pleaded with Elias to escort Diana to events. Their father would have come to town if Diana accepted a marriage offer, but that hadn't been necessary.

While Elias was glad his sister hadn't settled regarding her choice of husband, it also meant that he would have to repeat his role during the next season, and then again for Jenny and Grace when they were of age. It was a tedious task, when he'd much rather partake in far more pleasurable entertainment instead of standing in stuffy ballrooms.

"Have you ever known me to be merry?" Elias asked, smirking.

"From the satisfied grin on your face when you departed from that busty redhead last night, I'd say you made quite merry indeed."

Elias laughed. Jude wasn't wrong about that. "Well, we shan't have an opportunity for such engagements until after the holidays."

"Come now, Elias. There is a tavern in the village. We shouldn't have to live like monks for so many days."

"You make a fair point. Assuming we can escape from Diana and whatever she has planned for us." His sister had always dealt with her grief by keeping busy. Elias still couldn't believe his father agreed to allow her to host a big holiday house party. Their Aunt Penny helped her with the arrangements, although Elias doubted his sister needed the help at all.

Diana was better at estate management than even Elias was. She expressed an early interest, and their father taught the two of them together. It was Diana who managed their household with almost the same care and precision that their mother had, and she could oversee everything with the estates from ledgers to crop rotations to coordinating necessary building improvements.

"Do you know who all we will be subjected to at this event?" Jude asked. Jude may be a rake, but he had rules. One of those was not to dally with anyone from the *ton*, even the widows. Elias shared that rule after an encounter a few years ago went awry and made things quite awkward for him once he began escorting his sister to events.

Elias shrugged. "I didn't ask. Matt and Hudson will be there. And Hannah, of course. That is all I know."

Hudson and Hannah always spent the Christmas holiday with them. Their parents had also always joined them until Lord and Lady Onslow died a couple of years ago. So the friends all leaned on each other to cope with their grief. They had all been so close that it was almost like Elias had lost another set of parents.

"Stay away from dark alcoves and kissing balls." Jude teasingly wagged his finger at Elias.

"Now you sound like Hudson."

Jude chuckled and shifted his hands from behind his head to his lap. "I might eat my own hat if he cracks a smile even once during the entire party."

Hudson had always been the most serious among them. It has been something they teased him about during their time at university. He became even more so when his parents passed. Elias hoped his best friend might find something in life that would bring him a bit of joy one day.

"It depends on how often he's subjected to Matt," Elias said. Matt and Hudson were opposites in almost every way and the divide became worse after they had some falling out. But they could at least tolerate each other as long as they didn't have to spend too much time in each other's presence—or find themselves alone together.

"Perhaps it'll be a holiday miracle, and they'll resolve their differences," Jude said hopefully.

Elias scoffed. "I think there is a better chance that one of us takes a wife than Hudson embracing Matt as a friend again."

"Oof. So I shall make a different holiday wish, since we are committed to our bachelorhood."

"Good call," Elias replied. The years of watching how his father still missed Mama had hardened Elias's stance that he would never fall in love. Love would only bring pain and heartbreak. If he took a wife one day to do his duty to the title, it would be for an heir to continue his family line, and that would be all there was to it. And he wouldn't even consider doing so for many years.

The rest of the ride to Elias's family home in Sussex passed by quickly. The pair each took a nap in the carriage after their late night out, enjoying brandy, cards, and tending their respective needs with the willing women they had met.

Once the carriage rolled to a stop, and they both jerked awake. Elias glanced out of the carriage window, recognizing they had arrived at his family home. The men bounded from the carriage and were greeted by Elias's family. There was a bit of snow on the ground, and the air was crisp, instantly chilling his nose and ears.

"Good to see you, son," his father said, meeting him at the bottom of the steps into their expansive country home, grabbing him into a hug. His father had a bit of gray lining the edges of his hairline, but otherwise was still a fit, handsome man. He'd have no trouble taking another wife if he ever wished to do so, but he wasn't certain his father would ever look at another woman in such a way again.

Elias wasn't certain how his father did it, given that Elias was already questioning how he was going to make it so many days without a woman's touch. An outing to the tavern would be even more necessary, it would seem, even if he'd suffer the wrath of his sister if she caught them sneaking out.

His father moved on to greet Jude while Elias's sisters took turns hugging him. "Come, sisters," Elias said, noting their pink cheeks and noses. "Let's get inside before you all catch a chill."

They all entered the house, and Diana ushered them into the drawing room. She had asked Miller, their family's butler, to bring tea. Each of them took a seat, with Diana and Jenny sitting together on one settee, Papa and Grace sitting on the settee that faced them, and then Jude and Elias each taking high-backed winged chairs. Elias was positioned near his father, while Jude's chair was near Diana and Jenny.

"Now," Diana said, as if she were conducting a meeting of business. "Most of the guests shall arrive tomorrow, so I will need all of you prepared to greet them."

"I'm also a guest, am I not?" Jude asked, teasing her.

She rolled her eyes at him. "I suppose so. I arranged for you to be in your usual chamber. Your valet is already there unpacking for you. Hudson and Hannah will also arrive today, as well as Matt."

Jude smirked at her. "You are quite the hostess."

"Where is Aunt Penny?" Elias asked, glancing at the door. She was Diana's sponsor for the season, and her presence made it acceptable for Diana to play the part of a co-hostess, something an unmarried lady rarely did.

"She's taking a nap, but she should be down after a while," Diana replied.

A maid strolled in with the tea cart, placing it near Diana. His sister poured out for each of them, as she already knew how each of them took their tea. They remained quiet for several moments, enjoying the warm cup of tea in their hands and a saucer of tarts and biscuits.

"How many people did you invite to our home, sister?" Elias asked, shifting his attention to Diana.

"Ten, including their parents. Not counting all of you. Although, thanks to you and your friends, our numbers for unwed men and women will be even. We'll have five sets of those who are unmarried."

"Please tell me you aren't cooking up some kind of match-making scheme," Elias said, issuing a warning with his tone.

She waved him off. "I invited people I enjoyed during the season. Based on your reputation, I don't think any of them will be interested."

"Reputation for what?" Grace, who was only three-and-ten, asked.

"His inability to keep from mussing his cravat," their father said to Grace before casting an annoyed glance at Elias.

By the time his father got around years later to having the conversation he had promised about the birds and bees, Elias was beyond need of the explanation, having already partaken in such delights. Papa supported a young man sowing his wild oats, but with Elias aged six-and-twenty, his father believed it was about time to consider taking a wife.

Elias wasn't certain how his father could push him to marry so soon after the pain the man still lived with for the last twelve years. When Elias challenged him on the matter, his father always said that he would rather live with the pain than to have never had the time with his mama. Seemed far easier in Elias's mind to just avoid the whole matter entirely. At least until an heir became necessary.

"Well, I don't think you should marry a lady who cares so much about your cravat, brother," Grace said, raising her chin.

Elias grinned at her. "Quite right, sister." He shifted his focus back to Diana. "I had better not catch you sneaking off with any gentlemen you have invited." He narrowed his eyes, giving her the expression he'd used throughout the years when he needed to convey that he was serious and would brook no argument.

"I have already given her the same lecture," his father said before Diana could retort. "With you and your friends in attendance, I think she shall be well chaperoned."

"And as I already told Papa," Diana said in an annoyed tone. "I don't have interest in any of the invited gentlemen, nor do I wish to cause a scandal. We shall all have a happy Christmas."

"Hear, hear!" Jude exclaimed, raising his teacup as if he were toasting a fine brandy.

Elias raised his cup to join him, and they clinked their teacups together. Causing Diana to roll her eyes, and his father to chuckle.

The sooner they got the whole holiday behind them, the better. His contented bachelor life could return to normal. Well, perhaps it wasn't always a life of contentment, as it had its lonely moments, but a life of merriment was far better than the devastation that came from allowing one to succumb to the misery of love.

THE NEXT DAY, Diana was busy ordering them all about the house. Elias knew to pick his battles with his sister. He typically maintained the upper hand as an older brother and lord were rife to do, but there were times when it was in all of their best interest to take orders, and this was one of them.

Matt, Hudson, and Hannah had arrived the previous day as planned, which made for an entertaining dinner with all the banter and jabs at each other. He wasn't certain he'd seen his father laugh as hard or smile as much as he'd done in his place at the head of the table of chaos. It warmed Elias's heart to see more of the man his father used to be returned to them. He hoped that man would stay.

"Elias, there are carriages arriving," Diana called, pulling him from his thoughts. "We must line up to greet them."

They all donned their coats, and then Elias escorted Jenny and Grace on each arm, while their father escorted Diana to await the carriages.

"Your cravat doesn't look mussed," Grace said, giving him an approving smile.

He bit back his laughter, and they took their places.

They greeted their first guests, Lord Duncan and his mother. Diana sent them along with Miller to be shown to their chambers.

Another carriage wheeled up behind that one, and Elias did a double take, and then groaned when he saw who was being handed down. His father eyed him curiously, and Elias shook his head, willing his father not to call attention to his reaction.

Lady Billings caught his gaze as she made her way to where the family waited. Diana stepped forward, making the necessary introductions to everyone in the family.

"I believe we are already acquainted, my lord," Lady Billings said in a not-so-subtle way to Elias after Diana introduced them.

"Indeed. I hope you have been well, my lady," Elias replied, not lacking sincerity. He hoped the lady had been well. He would just have preferred not to be trapped in his family's home with her for a sennight.

Miller had returned and went to escort the widow to her chamber.

"Brother," Diana sighed, once Lady Billings was inside.

"Don't start, Diana." They didn't need to discuss such matters in front of their younger sisters. Hell, not with Diana either. "Why did you invite the woman, anyway? I'm not aware that the two of you are friends?"

Diana folded her arms across her chest. "She was kind to me during the season, and I thought she might make for pleasant company."

"I'm certain her kindness toward you was well intentioned," Elias said, not bothering to hide the sarcasm and disdain in his tone.

He glanced to his father for support and found the man's eyes crinkled at the edges where he fought his laughter.

"Father," Elias ground out.

"Come on, son. It's indeed quite funny."

He couldn't disagree more.

"Perhaps you should have warned me," Diana said, looking toward the other carriage making its way to their home.

"Perhaps you should have run your guest list by me," Elias challenged.

"Do we even want to know?" Jenny asked, watching them all with amusement.

Grace chimed in next. "Isn't it obvious, sister?" she asked, raising her chin as if she were a haughty debutante on the Marriage Mart. "The lady takes issue with our brother's cravats. Yours still looks perfect, brother. Pay the lady no heed." She paused as if she were contemplating something, then started again. "I don't think I like her at all."

They all fought their laughter, even Elias, as the next carriage arrived.

An older gentleman stepped out of the carriage, then turned to hand down a woman of similar age, although still quite pretty. Elias assumed the woman was his wife, as he hadn't met them before. The man reached back up toward the carriage opening and handed down another lady.

Something struck Elias when he saw her, causing him to steady himself. She had dark brown hair that he would have almost thought was black if he hadn't seen her in the daylight. Her skin was a creamy alabaster shade, and her perfect heart-shaped face was made even more beautiful with her light eyes. He couldn't quite tell the shade from where she stood, but just that they were a light color, which contrasted perfectly with her dark hair. She carried herself with a confidence that intrigued him, since she didn't appear to be much older than Diana.

His father cleared his throat, and Elias glanced at him to find him smirking.

Elias huffed and glanced back at the perfect, far-too-attractive miss approaching with who he could safely assume were her parents. Especially given how much she favored the older woman with her.

Diana greeted the older couple. "Lord and Lady Cary, I'm so glad you could join us."

She shifted her attention to his beauty. No, not his. Never his. He just thought she was beautiful. That's it.

"Miss Cary," Diana continued. "It's so good to see you again."

Diana turned toward the rest of them and introduced them all to Viscount Cary and his family. Elias was the first to step forward and take the perfect Miss Cary's hand, bringing it to his lips and placing a light kiss on her glove.

His heart raced, and he wasn't certain why. But he couldn't take his eyes off hers. Gray—the color of her light, mesmerizing eyes, was gray.

She pulled her hand from his, more like jerked it away, and gave him a tight, polite smile. "Nice to meet you, my lord."

He couldn't help but notice that when she went to greet his younger sisters, her expression was far more genuine, and pleasant. What was she about?

Once everyone had made their greetings, Lord Cary and his family followed Miller inside to settle into their chambers. Elias watched them, unwilling to admit to himself that he hoped Miss Cary might turn back to glance at him. She had been less than interested in him, and it only made him all the more curious about her.

As soon as their guests were inside and the door closed, his father released a stream of chuckles.

Elias jerked his head toward his father, irritated that he was almost certain that his father was laughing at his expense.

"Oh, son," his father said, controlling his laughter. "This is going to be so much fun."

"And just what is that supposed to mean?"

His father clutched Elias's shoulder. "You'll figure it out."

Elias rolled his eyes. His father had lost it. One step away from Bedlam. That was the only explanation.

CHAPTER THREE

Lydia

Miss Lydia Cary knew she'd end up spending a sennight alongside some of the biggest rakes of the *ton* when they received their invitation to the Snowdon holiday house party. But she had found that encountering Lady Diana's brother, Viscount Snowdon, in person had been something she hadn't been prepared for. Lady Diana became a fast friend when Lydia met her during the season at a garden party, but she had been all too pleased that she had avoided an introduction to the sworn rake.

It was obvious why he was a notorious rake, given he could drive a woman to distraction merely from looking at her. But she knew better. And wouldn't allow herself to be deceived by such charms again.

She knew exactly how dangerous a devilish man like Viscount Snowdon could pull willing women into his web, and she wouldn't allow herself to get ensnared by such a bounder again. She shuddered to think what it would have been like to end up trapped forever in marriage to a man who would have used her body and then taken up with every other willing light skirt in England.

But there was no harm in looking, right? She could still allow herself to admit that the viscount was indeed quite handsome. His light chestnut hair was just a tad longer than was proper, only adding to his rakish allure. Damn him. It was the deep blue eyes that shone like sapphires that were almost enough to render her speechless. Well, that wasn't exactly true. His broad shoulders also had something to do with it. Even in his greatcoat, she could see how well he filled it out. There wasn't a doubt that he possessed a taut form beneath all of his layers of clothing.

She shook off her woolgathering about the viscount, reminding herself that such thoughts would only lead to trouble. And she didn't want to be dallied with by the likes of him. She wished to find a man with more depth. One capable of love. And a husband that would respect and honor their vows. Even if a love match was too much to hope for, she would at least expect that her husband could remain faithful. Something that men like Viscount Snowdon were incapable of.

Lydia followed behind her parents as they ascended the grand staircase. Once they reached the top, the Snowdons' butler took them to the right. He showed her parents to a room on the left side of the hall, and then she was shown to a room on the right, across the way from her parents.

Entering the chamber she would call home for several days, she found a roaring fire set in the fireplace, making the room already feel warm and cozy. She fell across the four-poster bed, staring up at the canopy, pushing aside frustrating memories of Clint. Lydia had given little thought to the worst bounder of the *ton* in months. Not after she cried off from their engagement, and he disappeared.

But the handsome viscount downstairs made her body recall things. Things like the hint of pleasure that she hadn't realized her body was capable of, until she allowed the wrong man to touch her in the most scandalous, private of places.

With any luck, the blackguard was still at one of his family's Scotland estates, where he ran off to after her father threatened him if he didn't walk away quietly and leave her be.

The upside to the situation was that she had learned before it was too late. The rest of the *ton* was none the wiser that she had ever considered marrying the man, and Lydia had been spared a marriage where she would turn the other cheek while her husband was the worst sort of unfaithful arse.

Although, since then, her marriage prospects had been non-existent. She supposed she only had herself to blame, as she couldn't bring herself to get too close to any man. Nor had any intrigued her enough to consider getting over her fear that they would just lie to get at her virtue and her dowry.

"My lady," her maid, Tilly, said from the doorway, pulling Lydia from her thoughts. "Are you ready to change and freshen yourself after the long journey?"

"Yes, please. Thank you, Tilly."

Lydia climbed out of the bed as Tilly crossed the threshold and closed the chamber door behind her. Half an hour later, Lydia donned a fresh day gown and had her hair redressed. She took one last look at herself in the mirror, pleased with her appearance, and then exited her chamber to join the rest of the guests. Her parents' chamber door was closed, and instead of knocking to see if they were ready to join her, she decided she would venture downstairs on her own.

Once she reached the bottom of the staircase, a footman showed her to the drawing room, where some of the other guests had already gathered. The warmth from the roaring fire in the enormous fireplace reached her cheeks as soon as she entered. It made the room feel quite cozy, with the snow flurries falling outside the window.

She spotted Lady Hannah by the window and moved across the room to join her. Lady Hannah was the Earl of Onslow's sister and Lady Diana's closest friend. Lydia had met both of the ladies when they made their come outs during the last season. Neither of them had declared a betrothal, and she'd enjoyed getting to know them better during the house party.

"I love the snow, don't you, Lady Hannah?" Lydia asked, joining the lady's side.

"Indeed. It's quite beautiful," Hannah replied, giving her a kind smile. "And please call me Hannah, as many in attendance will."

"I will do so, if you call me Lydia."

Hannah looped her arm through Lydia's. "Of course. I shall be delighted to have your company since Diana will be so busy tending to all of her guests."

"I was quite surprised she was hosting this house party at all, especially as an unmarried lady."

Hannah's expression turned somber. "This is a time of year saddled with many memories, some not so pleasant. I believe she wishes to distract herself and the family from such sadness." Hannah leaned closer to Lydia. "Especially after having to experience her first season without her mama, and at the mercy of her brother, to chaperone her."

Lydia eyed Hannah curiously. "Wasn't it much the same for you?" She was almost certain that both of Hannah's parents had passed unexpectedly a couple of years ago.

Hannah gave her a somber nod. "Yes. Which is why I understand her reasoning. Diana's aunt Penny and our friend Juliana's mother, Lady Morley, sponsored us for the season. Then Elias and Hudson attended every evening entertainment with us, along with Matt and Jude. We were thankful for morning calls and garden parties for the chance to escape our brothers."

"You must also miss your parents very much," Lydia said, giving her a sympathetic smile.

"I do, of course," Hannah said, glancing around the room to see if anyone might overhear them. "But this time of year, we are most reminded of the loss of Diana's mama. You see, our families have always been the closest of friends. I was here as a girl when Lady Snowdon passed, and it wrecked us all."

Lydia frowned. "So she passed around this time, then?"

Hannah nodded, her eyes turning watery, but she held back her tears before drawing a deep breath. "Diana and I were only six then. We had played dress up and had tea with Lady Snowdon, just the three of us, not long before she passed. It shall always be one of my fondest memories."

Lydia noticed Viscount Snowdon standing across the room, speaking with some of his gentlemen friends. She couldn't help but wonder how the loss of his mother had affected him.

"Was your chamber comfortable for you, Miss Cary?" a distinct voice said, capturing her attention.

Jerking her head toward the newcomer, she noted Lady Diana now stood on her other side. "Yes, my lady. Quite."

"None of that, please just call me Diana," Diana said. "I am certain Hannah has said the same."

Lydia giggled. "You are correct. And please call me Lydia." Lydia was almost jealous that the pair had such a close friendship. Lydia had a few friends, but none as close as Diana and Hannah appeared to be. Young ladies on the Marriage Mart often made use of their hidden claws.

Diana grinned at them and then leaned a bit closer. "Did I tell you that Elias had the audacity to offer a string of threats if I should sneak off with a gentleman, and then I overheard him and Jude speaking about sneaking out to the village?" Diana directed her question to Hannah, but then glanced at Lydia as if seeking a reaction.

"Sounds typical to me," Hannah said, rolling her eyes.

"Is your brother much the same way?" Lydia asked, directing her question to Hannah. She wanted to have something to contribute to the conversation.

Hannah shrugged. "I have no idea. Hudson isn't the warmest or most forthcoming man. He's always been a good brother, but he confides nothing in me," she said. It was clear that the declaration saddened her. "What I know is that he will join the gentlemen if they should sneak out if there is even the slightest chance of him being left alone with Matt."

"Matt will be right there with them," Diana said quickly. "He's one of them."

"He's not the same as they are," Hannah said, defending Matt's character, or Lord Wilton rather.

Lydia watched both of them, intrigued by the inner workings of their deep friendships. Such relationships weren't a regularity among the *ton*, where titles, standing, and gossip governed the behaviors of most.

"Why wouldn't your brother wish to be alone with Lord Wilton?" Lydia asked, deciding it might be better to shift the conversation.

"We don't know," Hannah replied. "They were friends when they were younger, but they don't get along now. It seemed more on Hudson's account than Matt's, but none of the men will tell us why."

That was interesting. And interesting that both men still tolerated each other for the benefit of their other friends.

"And so much for what we heard about Elias and Jude's 'rules' too," Diana said, then lowered her voice. "It appears Elias had some kind of arrangement with Lady Billings."

Lydia jerked her head toward Diana and fought to soften her expression, hoping Diana wouldn't notice her reaction. Lady Billings was a young, pretty widow who captured the attention of many men, especially those who weren't marriage-minded. It shouldn't surprise her that he would take up with the woman, but something about the realization irritated her.

"You don't say," Hannah said, bringing her hand over her mouth, then dropping it back to her side.

"He wasn't happy when he learned she was a guest," Diana continued. "I wouldn't have invited her if I had known, of course. But Papa and I found it to be quite hilarious." Diana smirked and then glanced over at her brother for a moment.

Lydia didn't find the notion hilarious at all, which made no sense. He was nothing to her, and what difference did it make to her who he bedded? Lydia pushed off the thoughts and focused on how the siblings appeared to jab at each other. She often thought about what she had missed from not having any siblings of her own.

Glancing between them, Lydia studied the siblings. Even as

Diana mocked her brother to Hannah, it was obvious that she carried a deep affection and respect for him.

Suddenly, Elias glanced in their direction and caught Lydia's gaze. She hadn't even realized she still stared at him. A shiver jolted down her spine under his attention and she forced herself to remember that he had perfected his ability to control the affections of any woman with that very gaze, and she wouldn't fall prey to such a man again.

Chapter Four

Elias

Elias mentally chastised himself for how he continued to seek out the tempting Miss Cary. She already seemed to have become good friends with Hannah and his sister. Although, he supposed he shouldn't find that surprising, given that Diana had invited her to the party to begin with. He didn't recall seeing Miss Cary at any of the balls, or among Diana and her friends, so they must have met during daytime events when Elias had escaped to his club to recover from his late-night entertainment.

All throughout dinner that evening, he kept glancing at the lady when he believed she wasn't looking. She sat near Matt, and they appeared to be in conversation the entire meal. It irritated him to no end, and he'd have to gauge his friend's interest once he could get Matt alone.

He wasn't certain why he cared. She was an attractive woman, and that was that. He was a warm-blooded man who rarely went for long without a woman beneath him, so of course he took notice when one of the most beautiful women of the *ton* crossed his path. Well, not just crossed his path, but was also sleeping under his roof.

The realization did nothing to ease the tension that he carried in his shoulders, among other places. A trip to the tavern appeared to be in order. If only to get his mind off of the innocent marriage-minded miss who would be laid in a bed in the guest wing of his home—far too close to his own chamber—for the next several nights.

If there was one thing he had learned, he didn't dally with members of the *ton*, nor did he dally with innocents. He glanced down at the other end of the table and caught Betsy, Lady Billings, staring at him. Based on the heat in her expression, she wasn't harboring pure thoughts. Another reason he no longer thought of her as Betsy, and she was only Lady Billings to him. He had tried to put the formality back in their acquaintance, but she hadn't made things easy.

He shifted his gaze again and caught Diana's, who gave him a knowing look. Elias fought not to roll his eyes. The events were just another reminder of why he had rules, and why he would depart back to Town as soon as his sister's party had concluded.

He noted how Jenny whispered to Grace about something, and then Grace covered her mouth to hide her giggles. Jenny caught Elias watching them and then straightened a bit in her chair with a wide look in her eyes before giving him a one-shouldered shrug. He was almost certain she had said something about him. The younger girls would be allowed to attend some meals with the rest of the party and a few of the activities but would be with their governess directly after dinner. It was the agreement they'd made with Papa since the girls weren't out in society yet.

Elias decided that making eye contact with any of the women at the table wasn't in his best interest, so he kept his eyes trained on his plate while maintaining a bit of conversation with Hudson, seated to his right. If Hudson had dalliances, he kept them to himself and, in turn, stayed out of such awkward situations. Smart man.

When dinner ended, the gentlemen hung back to enjoy their port while the ladies departed to the drawing room. Elias knew that when the men joined them, they would find that Diana had set up some kind of game to force everyone to play. It had been like that at Christmas for many years. Diana always fought to keep all of them busy so they wouldn't have time to miss their mother.

He understood why she did so, especially for the benefit of their father, but sometimes Elias just wanted to miss his mother. He wanted to remember her and speak about her. They had all been too afraid to upset their father that they hardly spoke about her. Jenny and Grace couldn't even remember their mother, and how would they if he and Diana didn't tell them what she was like?

So far, all they know is that she was a beautiful woman from the paintings that were done of her, and that she loved horses. They mostly know that second part because of their father's aversion to allowing any of them to ride. Elias had learned before his mother passed, but didn't get to practice often unless he was away from his father, given how much any of his children riding upset the man.

Father had been adamant that the girls wouldn't learn to ride at all, much to Diana's dismay. She pleaded with him several times, to no avail. One of the few times Elias had argued with his father had been over horseback riding, so he found it easier to just avoid the topic altogether in his father's presence.

"She was watching you," Jude said, capturing Elias's attention when he moved to the seat on Elias's left.

Confused, Elias narrowed his eyes. "Who?"

"Lady Billings," Jude said, with a tone that conveyed it should have been Elias's first guess. "Who else?"

Elias waved him off, masking his disappointment. It would have been far more intriguing if Miss Cary had taken notice of him. Even though nothing would come of it, he could still imagine what the miss might be like. And he didn't want Lady Billings giving him a minute's thought. "I hoped she would have moved on by now. Why don't you fall on the sword, as it were, and keep her occupied?" Elias asked, nudging Jude's shoulder.

Jude didn't bother to temper his chuckle. "So that I can have her pining after me? I think not. I warned you not to dally with women of the *ton*."

"I recall," Elias said through gritted teeth. He didn't need the reminder. Another reason that even fantasizing about the beautiful Miss Cary was likely a terrible idea.

Jude brought his drink to his lips and swallowed. "But I shall join you when you wish to venture to the local tavern."

Elias took a healthy swig of his own drink, swallowing the burn of the amber liquid. "Soon. Tomorrow, perhaps." Escaping from the women of the house would provide a much-needed reprieve.

"That Miss Cary is a delightful conversationalist," Matt said, moving to join them. He almost took the seat in front of Hudson, then thought better of it and shifted a couple of seats down to sit across from Jude.

And the mention of Miss Cary again caused Elias to lose control of his face, allowing his annoyance to show. How was he going to overcome his obvious attraction to her? And if Matt intended to set his cap at her, that would certainly impede the things Elias had planned for her in his thoughts later.

"Oh, don't tell me that you are smitten, Matt?" Jude teased him.

Hudson perked up his ears at that, and Elias was thankful that it was Jude who broached the subject.

"No," Matt scoffed. "Nothing like that. She just didn't simper and enjoyed discussing the latest news. It was comparable to speaking with Diana or Hannah."

Hudson balled the hand resting on the table into a fist. Elias assumed it was the informal address of his sister, which had been another point of contention between the pair.

"I'm sure we will all look forward to getting to know her better," Elias said quickly, before Hudson could say something odious. Even if it caused his friends to cast him curious glances.

Elias continued, "I just mean that if she is a friend of our sisters," he motioned between himself and Hudson, "she will likely be among their group of friends we accompany to the events."

That seemed to pacify their curiosity, and Jude changed the subject to speak about the evening that he and Elias had before they arrived at the party.

Perhaps it was the nearness to the anniversary of his mother's passing, but recalling their conquests irked him a bit. It couldn't be for any other reason than that.

Once the gentlemen had all finished their port, his father directed them all to join the ladies in the drawing room. Elias went straight for the sideboard, giving himself a healthy pour of brandy and avoiding eye contact with anyone.

"Gather around everyone," Diana addressed the room. "We shall play charades."

Elias inwardly sighed. Couldn't the ladies just sing or something? His sister would no doubt keep them all busy with nonstop games and activities.

"We will divide into two teams. The ladies on one team and the gentlemen on the other. If the ladies win, they will get to select their partners for an activity tomorrow, but if the gentlemen win, they will do the selecting."

Elias scanned the room and noted that Lady Billings stared at him, a smirk playing on her face. He was suddenly far more invested in ensuring the men were victorious, if only so he could make certain that he didn't end up with the unrelenting widow as his partner.

He refilled his glass and moved to the area of the room where the men had congregated. Elias had always excelled at parlor games, and so did Matt and Jude. But Diana and Hannah were spirited competitors, so the ladies wouldn't make it easy for them.

The ladies took the first turn, and they selected Diana to act out a cue first. The ladies quickly guessed "Father Christmas" before the men could steal the point. Matt went next, and the men guessed "snowman," earning them the point and tying the game.

Elias flashed his sister a smirk, her attention to detail in theming all of their activities after the Christmas holiday wasn't lost on him.

They continued the game in that fashion for a few more rounds, keeping the game tied. The men had stolen a point from the ladies, pushing them ahead, but then the ladies stole one back.

Miss Cary got up to take her turn. She pulled a piece of paper from the vase on the table and then began attempting to act out the word, her eyes remaining locked where the ladies sat.

Knowing what the answer was, Elias called it out. "Angel."

She locked eyes with him, frowning, disappointed that the women had lost the point. *Not the most angelic reaction*, he thought, amusing himself. Evidently, she too had a competitive streak. He enjoyed that in a woman. Not that it mattered, of course.

Elias took his turn next, drawing a breath before he pulled his own slip of paper. He locked eyes with Jude, willing him to read his mind. They must maintain their lead. Elias began to dramatically move his hands.

"Handbells," Jude called just a second before Miss Cary repeated the word.

"Yes," Elias said excitedly, pointing at Jude. They narrowly earned the point. The ladies groaned at the gentlemen maintaining their lead, and Elias fought to play the part of a good sport and not taunt his sister. They hadn't won yet. There was still one round left.

For the last round, the women earned their point, and it came down to the last piece of paper. If the ladies stole the point, it would be a tie game, and they'd have to come up with a tiebreaker. Hudson begrudgingly stood and moved to the table.

Elias groaned internally, as his friend wasn't one to put as much thought into such games. He could only hope that the women would have a hard time discerning Hudson's movements.

Hudson set the piece of paper down on the table and looked at the gentlemen as he drew an annoyed breath.

Elias focused on him, waiting for him to make his first movement. Hudson made a rounded circle with his hands and then wrapped his arms around himself and puckered his lips. Elias might have poked fun and laughed at him if it weren't crucial that they win the point. He thought for less than a second and then jumped to his feet. "Kissing ball!" he shouted.

Hudson pointed at him. "Correct."

Elias patted his friend on the back from the delight at their victory. He could ensure he wouldn't be paired with Lady Billings.

"It would appear that the gentlemen have bested us, ladies," Diana said, then narrowed her gaze at Elias. "This time." She addressed the rest of the room again. "The men shall make their partner selections after breakfast tomorrow. Since it grows late and I am sure you are all tired from your travels, I shall bid you all a good evening."

A smile of satisfaction spread across Elias's face as he noted Lady Billings was among the guests who departed the room for the evening.

He spoke with Jude and Hudson for another quarter hour, while Matt had joined Diana and Hannah's conversation. He longed for a day when the four men might be friends the way they were when they were boys, or that one of them would at least tell him and Jude what was worth all the hostility.

But he didn't see that happening anytime soon, so he might as well focus on the victory he had earned. He'd have to decide who he wished to partner with in tomorrow's activity. Diana could be a safe choice that wouldn't give any of the ladies the wrong idea, but Miss Cary was a far more tempting option.

Elias fought a yawn and decided he was ready to retire to his chamber. Better to get his rest since it was clear Diana would have them tied up in activities all day, and the men still planned to sneak to the village later that next evening.

He departed from the group and made his way down the corridor when someone grabbed his arm and pulled him into a small study. Catching his balance, he turned to see the vexing woman illuminated by the light of the low fire.

"There you are," she said, her tone equivalent to the purr of a cat. "I've waited all night to get you alone. I very much hope you will warm my bed tonight. No one is as good as you are."

Before he could move, even to close the door so no one would catch them alone together, she practically pounced on him, wrapping her arms around his neck and pulling his head down so her lips crashed into his.

"Lady Billings," he growled and pulled his head back, refusing to give her the satisfaction of speaking to her on familiar terms. He removed her hands from around his neck and held her in place, away from him. "We've been through this. There shall be no further dalliances between us."

"That's not what you said the last time you had me bent over a settee. Very much like the one there by the fire." She wriggled her hands free and bunched the sides of her dress, as if she would raise her skirts there before him.

"But it is what I said the last time we spoke," he replied. "Three years ago, I might add. And I don't care for you in that way, nor will I ever marry you."

"I'm over that, my devilish man. I have accepted that you won't marry. But a woman still has needs, and mine haven't been well tended since you stopped calling on me."

His jaw clenched so hard his temples ached. He was beyond done dealing with the woman, nor did he have any desire to bed her again. His flaccid cock was a good indicator, and if he were feeling particularly vulgar and cruel, he'd make that point to her. He might enjoy bedding countless women, but he didn't appreciate being strong-armed in his family home, nor did he wish to relive the nightmare of dispensing her from his life the first time around.

"Find another willing gentleman to visit your bed," Elias ground out. "It won't be me."

He hurried away from her and left her alone in the room to

have whatever reaction she wished. He cared not, so long as she got the hint and left him alone. Hurrying up the stairs, he moved through the family wing of the house and locked his door behind him after he closed it, as he couldn't put it past the woman to determine where his room was and maul him in his sleep.

CHAPTER FIVE

Lydia

I F LYDIA WEREN'T already aware of what a cad that Viscount Snowdon was, the encounter she witnessed only proved her point. It had already irked that he had helped the men beat the women in charades, but then to overhear him and his lover only confirmed what she believed to be true of his character. They hadn't even bothered to close the door before his lips were on hers.

She had scurried away as soon as she saw his head lean down to kiss the woman, deciding she didn't wish to see or hear anything else. Lydia hoped they took the time to close the door before he lifted the woman's skirts, and before he scandalized his family with his behavior.

He probably fought so hard to win the game so that he could ensure he paired with the woman. Lydia supposed she shouldn't be surprised, since Lady Billings was a pretty widow with a bit of a reputation for sinking her teeth into the men known for their prowess. If the woman could land Jude, Viscount Sandon, the most notorious of them all, she'd have a complete set.

Lydia chastised herself for thinking such unkind things. It wasn't any of her business who the woman took to her bed. In the spirit of the Christmas holiday, she shouldn't be so harsh on others. Besides, the whole of the *ton* would call her a lightskirt if they knew she had also allowed herself to succumb to pleasure at the hand of a different rake.

As much as she hated the blighter, she couldn't deny that she enjoyed what he had done to her. Or what he had attempted to do when he touched the sensitive place between her legs. Even though she had stopped him since she didn't feel comfortable being so vulnerable with him, the touch had still awakened something within her. She had taken to repeating the act with her own hand, and had experienced something that made her shake and cry out in her chamber.

It didn't help that she heard Lady Billings proclaim what a remarkable lover that Viscount Snowdon was. She may not care much for the man, but she didn't doubt that he'd live up to his reputation in matters of bed sport.

She huffed and moved about her room, attempting to work off some of her pent-up energy.

There was a soft knock at the door and then Tilly cracked it open. "Are you ready for me, miss?"

"Indeed," she said more harshly than she had intended.

Tilly helped her to remove her dress and then don a serviceable night rail covered by a light blue dressing robe. Lydia settled in the chair before the mirror while Tilly brushed her long, dark hair and then fixed it into a long plait that fell over her shoulder. Fortunately, Tilly did most of the talking, and Lydia just listened.

The talk was mostly various *on dit* from other servants about their respective lords and ladies. It always amazed Lydia how the servants gossiped and got so much information from each other, which many of them undoubtedly shared, as Tilly had done. Gossip wasn't a sport limited to the members of the *ton*, it would seem.

Once Lydia had completed her evening ablutions, Tilly added another log to the fire, and then bid her goodnight. Lydia removed her robe and then crawled into bed. Warmth radiated within the bedding from where Tilly had put the bed warmer in place. Snuggling under the blankets, and bringing them to her chin, she pushed aside all of her thoughts and turned to her side, willing herself to fall asleep.

LYDIA'S EYES SHOT open, and she struggled to catch her breath. Her hand was between her legs with her night rail pulled up beneath the covers so that her hand worked the place at the start of her folds. Her chest rose and fell, as if she had sprinted across a field. She wasn't certain if she had actually achieved a climax, or if it had been part of her dream. Lydia supposed she didn't care, as the result was the same, and it had been even more intense than the first time she had experienced such a sensation.

She closed her eyes and saw him still there, touching her body. Lydia blinked her eyes open again, her cheeks heated. It would be quite embarrassing if Viscount Snowdon ever found out that she had dreamed of him and been driven to touch herself. He never would, given she would never tell another soul. She only hoped that her face wouldn't turn five shades redder when she saw him at breakfast.

The upside of the matter was that she relieved the tension within her body and perhaps she could finally put an end to such wicked thoughts. At least until she was back home, where she could imagine what the viscount looked like without his shirt on and not see him at the breakfast table.

Lydia had never seen a man without his clothes on before and would need to quit thinking about it if she wished the tension she had eased to remain at bay.

Climbing from her bed, she moved to the wash basin to wash her face, and her hands, after the way she had found herself once she woke. After she had freshened herself, she reached for the bellpull to ring for Tilly.

Half an hour later she was dressed in a pale blue morning dress, and her hair swept back into a simple chignon. Once Tilly had finished with her hair, she donned her ankle boots and then set off to join the others for breakfast.

She knocked on her parents' door this time. After she rapped her knuckles, her mother called from the other side of the door.

"Good morning, dearest," her mother said to her. "We were just about to join the others for breakfast."

"I shall walk with you then," Lydia said, bussing her mother's cheek.

Her mother put on a pair of earrings. "Did you sleep well?"

Lydia felt the blush hit her cheeks. "Very well." That wasn't a lie.

"Good." Her mother glanced over to where her father stood, his valet doing a last brush of his coat. "Ready, darling?"

Her father came over to where her mother was and extended his arm to her. "Indeed. I'm famished."

The tenderness between her parents warmed her heart. They had been a love match, and their love had only grown stronger in the many years of their marriage. Just another reason it would have been a travesty if she had been leg shackled to a man who desired to bed any woman, willing or unwilling.

After they exited the chamber, she took her father's other arm, and they strolled to the breakfast room. The scene was lively when they entered with the buzz of conversation around the table. There were only around fifteen guests invited, besides the Earl of Snowdon and his children, but it sounded like more as everyone excitedly chatted over their breakfast.

The sideboard had been set up with an array of offerings, so Lydia and her parents went there first to fill their plates and then find seats. Unable to stop herself, Lydia glanced around the table to see who was already there. As much as she loathed to admit it, she was looking for Viscount Snowdon, but didn't see him.

His father sat at the head of the table with Diana seated to his right, and her sisters lined up beside her. She noted that Lady Billings sat at the other end of the table. Lydia opted to take the seat across from Diana and beside the elder Lord Snowdon, deciding that the younger Snowdon would select the seat near his lover.

"I am so glad that you could join us, Lydia," Diana said after Lydia had taken her seat, and a footman helped to push her chair in.

"I am looking forward to seeing what other events you have planned. Your home is quite lovely."

"Thank you," Diana said, beaming with pride. "I have done my best to ensure that things have been well tended to over the years."

The elder Lord Snowdon closed his eyes for a moment and drew a deep breath, then forked a bit of eggs into his mouth.

Diana noticed and placed her hand on her father's arm. "I think you will like the activity I have planned for the morning, Papa," she said, her eager tone only slightly forced. "We are going to build snowmen. You, Jenny, and Grace shall be the judges."

Her father gave her a small smile and set his fork down to pat Diana's hand, then picked it back up again. "That sounds very nice."

Lydia's body heated when a gentleman swept into the room out of the corner of her eye. She didn't even have to look at him to know who it was. Training her eyes on her plate, she willed herself to focus on her breakfast. He was at the sideboard behind where she sat. Drawing a deep breath, she told herself that in only a few moments, he would be seated at the other end of the table, and she could forget that he had entered.

A few moments later, the empty chair beside her moved and the very man set his plate down beside hers. Once he took his seat, the intoxicating scent of sandalwood with a hint of cinnamon took over her senses. She wondered if he intentionally selected the scent for the holiday or if he usually wore a note of cinnamon. Not that it mattered, but if she were going to dream of him again, the added sensory details might enhance the experience.

She chastised herself for how wanton she had allowed her

thoughts to become. There would be no more imagining of the man. No good could come of that. Before she could argue with herself any further, he addressed the group.

"Father. Sisters," he said, giving them a nod. "Miss Cary, you look well this morning."

She noticed the elder Lord Snowdon had a small smirk playing at the corners of his lips, and she wasn't certain what it was about. But she was pleased to see that he at least appeared less grim.

"Thank you, my lord," she replied.

"I hope you were met with a comfortable bed after all the excitement of yesterday's events."

If she didn't know better, she might think the man knew her secret, but he couldn't. She was reading far too much into his words. She wanted to roll her eyes, even though he would not understand why she had done so. Nor was he aware that she knew all too well what comforts he had in bed the previous evening, likely not his own.

"I slept well," she said, giving him a polite smile.

"Brother," Diana said, saving Lydia from another comment from the man, "have you given thought to who you will ask to pair with you in the morning's activity?"

"Well, sister, I'm still deciding, as there are many fine choices, but I am giving thought to asking Miss Cary," he said, turning his head toward Lydia. She glanced at him and saw his smug expression, as if he were waiting to see if she might express delight over him teasing that he might give her the honor of his presence as a partner. Some honor.

Lydia grinned at him. "My lord, I am certain Lady Billings would be quite put out. She seemed to desire your attention far more than I."

The elder Snowdon and Diana bit back a laugh, and Diana had to resort to hiding behind her napkin. She wondered if they already knew about the arrangement he had with the woman.

"That's all well and good, but I don't wish to partner with

Lady Billings," he said, and she noticed his jaw clenched when he did so.

"Brother," Grace said from across the table, "fix your cravat." His youngest sister gave him a knowing look, and the rest of the Snowdon family fought laughter again. Lydia didn't understand what was so funny, so she glanced at Viscount Snowdon's cravat for some kind of clue, and it was only slightly tilted out of place. He straightened it and he took a bite of egg.

The way his jaw flexed when he chewed only made her more aware of the masculine lines of his face and his perfect, aristocratic nose. His lips were full, and she imagined they were quite soft. Great, she thought to herself. Even his chewing brought on wanton thoughts.

She wasn't certain she could be trusted to be near the man, especially if she didn't wish for him to keep appearing in her dreams. "Well, I'm not certain I will partake in the activity. Perhaps I shall set off on a ride about your estate."

The elder Lord Snowdon rose from his chair. "If you all will excuse me."

Diana glanced toward her father as he walked away and then to her brother, sadness marring her expression.

"I'll go to him," Elias said, dabbing his lips with his napkin and then setting it aside. He rose from his chair and hurried after his father.

"I'm sorry," Lydia asked, confused at what had occurred. "Did I say something wrong?"

Diana gulped. "No, of course not," she started. "It's just that..."

"Our mother died from falling off her horse," Grace said, finishing her sister's thoughts. "I was just a baby."

Lydia gasped, realizing her error.

"And today is the anniversary of her passing," Diana said, the pain evident in her tone. "We lost her twelve years ago."

Lydia brought her hand to her mouth and fought the tears that formed in the corners of her eyes. "Please accept my apologies. I had no idea, otherwise I would never have suggested a ride." She immediately felt sorry for both the Lords Snowdon, but her mind especially drifted to the viscount.

She shouldn't have jabbed at him and should have just accepted his request to partner with her if that is what he chose. If he ended up asking her, she would agree and would be an amiable partner. Although, she still wasn't certain why he wouldn't pair with Lady Billings instead, based on what she witnessed.

Diana nodded and sighed. "You have nothing to be sorry for. Papa shall never cease grieving for Mama. I suppose the same for the rest of us." Diana shifted her expression to a small smile and glanced at each of her sisters. "But we are going to have a fun day, as Mama would have wanted. Right, sisters?"

Jenny and Grace nodded, and everyone refocused on their breakfast plates.

Grace broke the silence. "Lydia," Grace said, "May I call you Lydia? I know Diana does."

"Of course," Lydia replied. "I would be honored if you did so."

"You may call me Grace," their youngest sister said.

Lydia found she already liked the young girl very much. She was certain to keep the entire family on their toes when she came of age.

"Thank you, Grace," Lydia said, giving her a polite nod.

"Lydia," Grace started again, "Do you take issue with mussed cravats?"

Lydia eyed her curiously, while Diana and Jenny's shoulders shook from their laughter.

"I don't believe so," she replied, unsure if there was a right or wrong answer to the question. She glanced at the older sisters and they both had their mouths covered with their hands. "I suppose things happen sometimes to muss them."

"That's an excellent answer," Grace said, giving her the sweetest grin.

"Do I want to know what this is about?" Lydia asked, glancing at Diana and Jenny again.

They both shook their heads.

"I like you, Lydia," Grace said.

Lydia was still quite confused but smiled at Grace. "I like you too."

She did not know what had just occurred, but something about earning young Grace's approval made her happy, even if she didn't understand why.

CHAPTER SIX

Elias

ELIAS DID HIS best to offer his father a bit of comfort after following him to his study. Miss Cary had said nothing wrong, and she was surely confused over the situation, which made Elias feel bad for departing without a word. Diana would explain things to her, he hoped.

Papa struggled the worst with Mama's passing around the holidays. Which only supported Diana's theory that if she filled the house with love and laughter that it would help them all to get through it.

Once he managed to get his father to speak, the pair reminisced about Mama for a moment, and then Elias lightened the mood by telling his father a few more stories about his antics with Jude.

"You need to open your heart to the idea of love, son," his father finally said.

"Are you mad? Do you see the pain that you still suffer even all these years later? Why would I risk that pain on myself, or worse, on someone that I would love and care about if something should happen to me?"

Tears formed in his father's eyes again. "Son, as saddened as I am to continue on without your mother, I have never wished for a second to have not had her for the time that I did. I would choose our life together even if I had known how things would end."

"But now I know better, Father. If I don't allow it in, I don't have to risk such a fate."

"You will marry sooner or later. I know you believe in your duty to the title and our family," his father said.

"Father, I know it's been a while for you, but love isn't required to marry and sire an heir. And I believe, based on the many stories I have recounted to you, that you are already well aware that I am more than capable of doing the needful activities."

His father's face hardened. "Don't be so crass about such things, Elias. I promise you that you will cheat yourself out of the life you deserve if you take that approach to marriage. There is nothing like looking into the face of your children and seeing the woman you love in them. Knowing that a piece of them will continue to live on for generations and generations. It's a much stronger feeling and sense of pride than carrying on these blasted titles."

"I don't think I can," Elias said, his chest rising and falling from where his breathing rate increased, and attempted to push aside what his father said. Especially how it made him question his resolve. "I just don't think I can let myself love someone, Father."

"You already have, son. You loved your dear mama, and you love me. And you love your sisters," his father said, then grinned at him. "Most of the time. You are capable of love, son. I'm not asking you to go out and force yourself to fall in love with the first woman you see, but I am asking you to be open to it."

Elias contemplated what his father said. He still had his doubts, and the whole notion of it didn't sound all that appealing. The fear of pain was still far too great.

"And about what you are doing with all of those women of the night, Elias. You take risks, to your health and to your future, in continuing down that path. It's one thing to sow your wild oats, but that time must eventually come to an end. And one day you're going to understand the difference between what you are doing with those nameless women and the love with the one woman you give your heart to."

For the first time in his life, Elias felt slightly embarrassed over his behavior. Something he'd never experienced before, given that he always saw it as something to brag about to the other gentlemen. But something about his father's words had him questioning everything he thought he enjoyed about his life and what he wanted for his future. And Elias couldn't stop himself from wondering what his mother might think of his actions.

He still wasn't convinced he wanted love or that love would have a place in his marriage, when he pursued one, but perhaps it was time that he gave what he wanted for his future a bit more thought.

His father clasped his shoulder. "I think we should rejoin the party before your sister comes looking for us."

Elias pushed aside his thoughts and grinned at his father. "We won't get a moment's rest until after Christmas."

"In that, I believe you are correct." His father laughed, and then caught Elias's attention again. "That reminds me, son. Did you need anything from the attic? I have the servants going through some of your mother's things for Diana."

"I don't believe so."

"Very well," his father replied. "Let me know if you think of something."

They departed his father's study and returned to find that the guests had gathered outside, dressed in their great coats and winter coverings. Elias and the elder Lord Snowdon donned their warm coats and joined the others out in the snow.

Elias left his father's side and went straight to Miss Cary. After the way he departed and their awkward conversation at breakfast, he knew he should at least let her know that all was well with his father, or at least as well as it would ever be.

He noted Lady Billings looking around as if she were searching for someone. As cowardly as it might have been, he ducked behind Jude and then continued to where Miss Cary stood.

"Miss Cary," he started, "I see you decided to join the morning's activity."

She turned to face him, and her gray eyes bore into his with a flicker of remorse.

"Lord Snowdon, please accept my apologies for earlier," she blurted.

He waved her off. "You have nothing to apologize for. My father is back enjoying time with the other guests," he said, motioning toward where his father stood, ironically chatting with Miss Cary's parents. "Are you perhaps unclaimed for the activity? If so, I would like to select you to be my partner."

She grinned at him, and it was the kindest expression she had shown him since she had arrived. "Then it appears I shall partner with you, my lord."

"Given our mutual spirit of competition, I don't think the rest of this lot stands a chance. What say you?" Elias said, extending his arm so she could take it.

"I do quite enjoy winning," she said, taking his proffered arm. "I don't think I could stomach another loss."

"Well, then, my lady, I'll do my best to ensure you won't face a crushing defeat."

Diana got everyone's attention, and they all gathered around as she explained the rules. Then Aunt Penny explained what the judges would look for to determine the winner. There would be five different teams: Elias and Miss Cary, Diana and Jude, Hudson and Hannah, Matt and Miss Stone, and then Duncan and Lady Billings. Each team would have two hours to work on their snowman, and the one that was deemed the most creative would be awarded a prize. The teams could use anything they could find outside, and were only given a pair of cutters they could use to cut twigs.

The time limit should give them plenty of time to plan their design and then gather the materials that they would need, depending on how complex their build turned out to be.

Lady Billings caught his eye and gave him a scowl as she looked between him and Miss Cary on his arm. The lady stood near Lord Duncan, a viscount that Elias was almost certain would be more amenable than he was to the arrangement the widow sought. Perhaps she would take up with Duncan and leave Elias alone. It would be a Christmas miracle, indeed.

Aunt Penny declared the start of the competition and the couples spread out to discuss their plans where they wouldn't be overheard. Elias noticed that Hudson and Hannah were already bickering and chuckled to himself. He knew that given the choice, Hudson would choose to partner with his sister, if only to avoid tedious conversation with another chit. But given the way Hannah was arguing with him, Elias wondered if Hudson had noted the folly in his choice.

"Do you have any ideas, Miss Cary?" Elias asked, lowering his voice so only she could hear him.

"I was thinking," she started, "what if we make a scene instead of just making a single snowman?"

"What do you mean?"

She stepped closer to him, and his body heated at the realization that he stood less than an inch away from her feminine body brushing against his. When she leaned her head forward so her lips were so close to his ear that he could feel the heat of her breath, it would have been so easy to turn his head and allow their lips to meet. Instead, he drew a deep breath and forced himself to remain still.

"What if we build two snowmen, or even a snowman and a snowwoman, and have them in a scene together?"

"Ah, I see what you mean. What could we have them do?" He tried his best to think of an idea, but his rational thought had left his body with her so painfully close to him. His father's words from earlier reverberated in his head, but he quickly shoved those aside. She was a beautiful woman, and of course, his body should notice. The rapid beat of his heart meant nothing.

"I've got it," she said excitedly. "We'll have them kiss, under mistletoe."

He grinned at how excited she was about the idea. "Let's do it. I think I can make it look like the mistletoe is hanging above them."

She started rattling off the things that they would need. Various twigs and rocks that would be used in different places. She had designs on how they would fashion a dress for the snow woman. They would also have to venture out in search of a sprig of mistletoe and a long stick for Elias to position it so that it hung over their creation.

Both pleased with their plan, they set off to gather the things they would need. They found the different stones first and then brought those back to the area where they had claimed to build their scene.

Miss Cary had such excitement for the activity, and Elias found it catching. He too was smiling and excitedly held up sticks he thought would suit their plans. Then he'd almost puffed out his chest with pride when she gave him a satisfied nod. He couldn't remember the last time he'd had so much fun.

Before long, they had gathered all the different sticks and twigs they would need and had placed them with their other materials. Hudson and Hannah had already started building, with Hudson rolling a large ball of packed snow over to where Hannah waited. Matt and Miss Stone had also started their snowman, with their base in place and working to add some kind of elaborate detail around the bottom.

Elias glanced back to Miss Cary, and she grabbed his hand to pull him with her. Even through both of their gloves, he felt the warmth from her hand in his. He forced himself to look away from her and focus on their search. The last thing they needed to find was their sprig of mistletoe.

They entered the patch of trees at the edge of the open area where the teams were working, continuing into the trees until they were not visible to anyone else. He noted she hadn't released his hand, and he found he had no desire to let her go. Their hands seemed to fit together perfectly.

She continued to pull him through the woods, looking up as she did so. Her cheeks were pink from the cold, and when his eyes dropped to her lips, he noted those were also a similar shade. He licked his own lips in an instinctive response and allowed her to lead him deeper into the forest.

Miss Cary stopped and looked around, trying to decide where they would go next. Elias glanced at the branches above them and grinned when he saw the most perfect bundle of mistletoe directly over her head. The white berries were easy to spot against the green leaves.

"Miss Cary," he said, giving her a wide grin.

She glanced at him curiously, and he responded by pointing up above her head.

He was almost positive that her cheeks turned even darker when she realized where she stood. His cock took notice, twitching at the thought that he would taste her lips.

"It would be bad luck if I didn't kiss you," he said, stepping closer, her hand still in his.

She gulped. "I suppose you are correct."

He cupped her cheek with his gloved hand and gave her a soft smile before he lowered his head and brushed his lips against hers. The electricity that shot through his body was something he hadn't experienced in all of his six-and-twenty years. Needing to taste more of her, he ran his tongue along the seam of her lips. When she opened to him, he swept his tongue inside to meet hers.

To his surprise, she didn't back away or end the kiss, but deepened it, massaging her tongue against his. He released her hand and wrapped his arm around her waist, holding her tighter against him, the ridge in his breeches pressed against her midsection, since he was so much taller than she was.

Her gloved hands moved between them and pressed them flat against his chest, doing nothing to ease the intensity of the shockwaves he felt. He wanted more and feared that even that might never be enough from the way he drank from her. Elias imagined pushing her back against the tree and having her wrap her legs around his waist.

Perhaps she sensed he was losing his grip on his gentlemanly principles, because she broke the kiss and pulled away from him. He released the hold he had on her so she could take a couple of steps back.

"I got carried away," Elias quickly said. "Please forgive me." Although he wasn't certain why he was apologizing. He didn't feel bad about kissing her, and if she would allow him to do so again, he wouldn't be able to turn down the opportunity.

"No one saw us, so there is no need to speak of it again," she said, staring up at the mistletoe, as if she were unfazed by their kiss and ready to continue what they had ventured into the woods to do.

Elias tamped down his irritation. He didn't need her to fall at his feet or profess some promise of love, because lord knows he certainly wasn't going to, but it might have been nice if the kiss had some kind of lasting impact on her. "Very well," he said, deciding that there wasn't much else he could say unless he wanted to appear as some besotted fool, which he absolutely was not. "I shall cut down what we need."

Elias climbed the tree with ease and cut a few sprigs. He handed them down to Miss Cary, and then he climbed back down a few feet to the ground. Pushing aside the annoyance he still felt about how nonchalant Miss Cary had been about their kiss, he extended his arm to her, and they set off back out of the woods so they could begin crafting their scene.

His competitive nature only slightly helped him set aside the thoughts of how soft Miss Cary's lips were or how her tongue had tasted like tea and blackberry jam. They worked well together, even if he was constantly at war with impure thoughts of how pink her cheeks would look in contrast to the snow, if he were to lay her down in it.

They each checked over their scene as Aunt Penny announced that everyone's time was up. It turned out even better than he had expected. The scene itself was ironic, given what had occurred between them, and that he would happily haul her right back to the very spot and repeat the action.

For their scene, they had constructed two snow people with twig arms that reached for each other. Lydia had fashioned a dress for the snow woman from twigs and branches filled with pine needles. Elias had constructed a replica of a top hat on the snowman using sticks, and a cravat made from greenery. They had placed greenery around the base to make them appear as if they were standing on some kind of rug. Then they had used a long stick to hold up the mistletoe, which Elias had taken care to pack the supporting stick well, so that it would remain secure.

Elias glanced around at the competition and believed they stood a good chance at winning. They had been the only ones to build two snow figures for theirs. The dress and the greenery bonnet that Miss Cary created at least matched, if not exceeded, the detail the others had created.

His father and sisters began walking by each of the teams, assessing their snowmen. When they neared where Elias and Miss Cary stood, he extended his arm to her and they stood to the side, watching as his family looked over their scene. He beamed with pride when his sisters pointed out the details. Elias's father caught his gaze when Jenny pointed out how romantic the scene was, and Elias looked away, not wanting his father to read too much into it. The scene hadn't even been his idea.

The elder Lord Snowdon, Jenny, and Grace huddled together, and then, after several moments, they turned to face everyone. "You all did a wonderful job," his father started, "and it looks like you all had a lot of fun too. My daughter has already told me I cannot declare everyone the winner, so after reviewing the efforts from each team, we are ready to make our choice."

His father paused for dramatic effect and glanced between each team. "The winners are Miss Cary and Viscount Snowdon."

Diana stepped forward. "I shall inform you of your prize on Christmas Eve, the day after tomorrow."

The only person who appeared put out by the announcement was Lady Billings, who crossed her arms and rolled her eyes when Miss Cary expressed her delight over winning. Elias turned his back to the woman and congratulated his partner on a job well done.

He played with a bit of fire when he leaned toward her and whispered, "I'd ask for a kiss for the winner, but I believe we already anticipated our win."

Pulling back to gauge her reaction, he watched her cheeks pinken. But aside from the change in her skin tone, there was no reaction from her. The only upside to his disappointment was that it aided to keep his half-erection from increasing. He wasn't certain why her resistance to him drove him as mad as it did. He reminded himself that no more could occur between them, regardless.

Miss Cary was an innocent, not a woman to dally with, but a woman who would seek marriage. And just because he might let a bit of his father's lecture seep into his thoughts didn't mean that he'd marry anytime soon, which meant the tempting Miss Cary was off-limits.

CHAPTER SEVEN

Elias

ELIAS AND HIS friends snuck out that evening. After they were subjected to a few card games, the guests began departing for their chambers. They didn't invite Lord Duncan to join them, and Elias secretly hoped he would keep Lady Billings occupied so he didn't have to be on guard every time he passed an open doorway in his own home.

Jude, Matt, and Hudson had all been willing to escape the Snowdon home for a few hours. They most likely wouldn't have another opportunity to enjoy an evening out together until the season started in the spring, since they each had respective matters of business to attend to at their country estates.

If they could keep Hudson from scowling at Matt for just one evening, it might prove almost like old times when they visited taverns in their university days.

The busty tavern maid brought them each over a tankard of ale. Even Hudson didn't bother to hide that he took notice of her. Elias thought he almost saw a smile form on his friend's face, which was a rare occurrence, indeed. The woman glanced at Elias and then each of his friends, likely assessing them to determine which of them could be a likely customer for other matters of business.

The next thing he knew, the woman came around the table

to Elias and sat on his lap. "You will let me know if there is anything I can do for you this evening, won't you?"

Of all his friends, she would likely have had the best luck that evening if she had propositioned Jude. Although, Elias would be lying if he said he hadn't fucked a barmaid in an alley before. On more than one occasion.

His father's words and the disappointment in his eyes when he spoke about Elias's need to move past sowing his oats nagged at Elias. Particularly on the anniversary of his mother's death, as he could only imagine that she would have plenty to say about the way he had behaved the past several years.

Miss Cary's beautiful face flashed in his mind with her pink cheeks and perfect mouth, and that pushed him over the edge, even if he didn't understand why. He urged the barmaid to remove herself from his lap. "Not tonight, but I'm certain you won't be lonely," he said, nodding toward other tables of gentlemen.

She huffed and stormed off from their table. He released a deep breath.

"Are you feeling all right, Elias?" Jude asked, smirking at him. "Don't tell me you have suddenly become marriage-minded."

Jude knew good and well all the distasteful things that Elias had done, and vice versa.

Elias took a large gulp from his tankard and slammed it harder on the table than he intended. "It's the anniversary of my mother's passing. I'm just not in the mood."

His friends all glanced down at their ale. Jude had never met his own mother since she died giving birth to him. Hudson lost his mother at the same time as his father a couple of years prior. While Matt's mother was still alive, he hardly saw her since she spent most of her time on the continent.

"Your mother was a treasure, Elias. We all miss her," Matt said, giving him a small smile.

They each raised their glass and toasted her memory. Elias felt she would smile down on them if she could see that the four had remained such good friends. Well, aside from whatever trouble there was between Matt and Hudson. She'd have probably made them knock their shite off already.

An awkward silence fell over the group for a few moments.

"It's amazing you don't have any wounds from how much you and Hannah bickered today," Jude said, speaking to Hudson. "Don't you two ever give it a rest?"

Elias laughed and appreciated the change in the conversation. He hadn't meant to put a damper on their time out.

"She's the one that won't give it rest," Hudson ground out.

Jude glanced between Hudson and Matt several times, who sat across from each other at the table, then refocused his gaze on Hudson. "Please, tell me more."

"I'm her guardian. So what I say goes," Hudson said, waving Jude off.

"I think I understand perfectly," Jude said, laughing. "I'm utterly shocked to learn that she hasn't settled into the part of the biddable young lady." The sarcasm was thick in his tone, causing Matt and Elias both to erupt in hearty laughter.

Another voice broke into their banter. "I haven't seen the lot of you gents in a long time."

"Durham, what brings you to this part of Sussex?" Matt asked, motioning toward one of the open chairs.

Viscount Durham lowered himself into the seat between Matt and Jude. "Visiting Downe for the holiday," he said, motioning toward another gentleman they had all attended university with. At that moment, the man had the barmaid in his lap, and given his head was practically between the woman's breasts, it seemed he wouldn't turn down her services for the evening.

"What about all of you?" Durham asked.

"My sister is throwing a house party," Elias replied, "and we all decided we required an evening out."

Durham's eyes widened, "Can an unmarried lady throw a house party? Or did I miss the announcement in the papers?"

"My Aunt Penny is officially the one hosting it, I suppose, but it was my sister's doing," Elias said, hoping the man would not take an interest in Diana. From what he knew about Durham, he wasn't someone who Elias would allow anywhere near his sister.

"How interesting," Durham said. "Are there any compelling ladies in attendance?"

Jude laughed. "It depends on how you define compelling. Although Elias was all too pleased to see Lady Billings."

Durham started chuckling. "I heard Betsy had set her cap at you. Poor woman."

Given the informal reference Durham made to Lady Billings, Elias could only assume that he had also had an arrangement with the lady at one point.

"Perhaps she would enjoy your company, Durham," Elias said, hoping that if Lord Duncan didn't sway her, perhaps Durham would be another option to keep her entertained. She could sneak out of the party just as easily as they all had.

"I'll take that under advisement," Durham said, motioning to another barmaid to bring him an ale.

"Our sisters," Elias said, motioning between himself and Hudson, "and Miss Stone and Miss Cary are the only other ladies present, aside from a couple of married mamas."

Elias thought he saw a reaction on the man's face, but it was gone as quickly as he saw it, if so.

"Well, I hope you gents won't be too bored from all the parlor games and holiday activities. Downe and I will find us a couple of doxies to enjoy. Happy Christmas to us."

Elias hoped he never sounded like that or said anything of the sort. Although, if he were honest, he probably had. Perhaps not at Christmas, since he was always with his family, but other times for certain. Hell and damnation. His father's words wouldn't escape his mind, and he wasn't certain he'd be able to enjoy the rakish life he had led for so long.

Moving on from such a life didn't irritate him as much as he might have thought, but the uncertainty about what that would mean for his future and what he wanted for his life most assuredly did.

The barmaid returned and set down several tankards on the table. As soon as her hands were free, Durham cupped her arse and pulled her against him, seating her on his lap. "Are you going to climb on top of my cock tonight and show me what you can do?"

She hesitated and looked like she would remove herself from his lap, but he grabbed the back of her head. "Don't be shy in front of my friends here. Perhaps they might want to watch."

Fear marred her expression, and tears welled in her eyes. "Release her now, Durham," Elias ground out.

Durham sneered at him, but did as Elias had commanded. Elias motioned to Hudson that it was time to go. Matt and Jude followed suit, bidding Durham a curt farewell.

In an attempt to be polite and hope that Durham wouldn't take out any anger on the poor barmaid after they left, they pretended they might see each other at the tavern again another night. But Elias had no intention of ever associating with Durham.

Besides, even if they wanted to get out again, Diana was likely to keep them exhausted the closer they got to Christmas.

When they returned to his family estate, the men attempted to enter as quietly as they could so as not to wake the rest of the house. Jude, Hudson, and Matt all moved toward the staircase.

Elias hung back, not quite ready to go to his chamber, but also not really wanting one of his friends to join him. He'd only had a couple of tankards of ale, so he had all of his wits, but his defenses were down, and he continued to question everything he believed he wanted for himself.

He trudged to the library, hoping the fire was still lit and he might lie across the settee and lose himself in his thoughts.

When he approached, the library door was open, so he closed it behind himself, releasing an audible sigh. The fire was low and emitted little light, but the moon brightened the area around the windows where it had begun to snow.

Elias dropped himself onto the settee and massaged his temples. Suddenly, a shadow moved in the room.

"Who is there?" Elias asked.

For a moment, he suspected his eyes were playing tricks on him, but when he settled back down, something bumped into one of the tables.

"Show yourself," he called more sternly.

A feminine figure stepped forward from the shadows, and he knew who it was as soon as she stepped into the lit area from the moon.

Elias rose to his feet. "Miss Cary," he said, his voice more like a whisper.

"I-I couldn't sleep," she stammered. "I thought to find a book."

"Is your chamber not comfortable?" he asked, hoping she couldn't see that he eyed her form from head to toe. He couldn't fully see her but could see enough that she donned a dressing robe, which he did his best not to imagine what might lie beneath. Her bare toes poked out from under the garment, and his cock had a mind of its own, testing the integrity of the three buttons on each side, holding him at bay. His eyes continued wandering slowly back up her body.

She took a single step closer, and his entire body tingled from the awareness. "It's not that," she said with a sigh. Her hair was in a loose plait over her shoulder, and the urge to untie the ribbon and loosen her dark tresses almost took over.

"Then what is it?" he asked, his heart racing. He would do whatever he must to ease her mind and help her sleep. The realization only made his heart race faster and his breaths shorter.

"I...well..." she started, then shifted on her feet. Before he knew what was happening, she had closed the distance between them and had wrapped her arms around his neck, pulling his lips against hers.

He growled and placed his hands on her lower back, deepening the kiss. Part of him wasn't certain if he was actually dreaming. Perhaps he had fallen asleep watching the snow, and she appeared to him in his dream like an angel. If so, he wasn't ready to awaken.

Elias shifted one hand to her bottom, pulling her to her tiptoes and pressed her against the telling bulge he sported. She mewled into their kiss, pressing her tongue harder against his, and running her hand into his hair.

Bringing his other hand between them, he grazed his fingers across the globe of her breast. Breaking their kiss, he kissed along her jaw and neck as he cupped her breast in his hand.

She drew a deep breath. "Yes. My lord," she whispered.

"Elias," he whispered against her ear.

"Elias," she repeated.

The sound of his name on her lips almost made him come undone. But he regained control of himself and held both of his hands up, releasing her.

"I don't know what came over me, Miss Cary," he said. Although she had been the one who had kissed him, right?

She stepped against him again. "You have nothing to be sorry for," she whispered.

"I overstepped." Hadn't he just chastised himself that very evening for his rakish behavior and then there he was mauling an innocent miss in his family's library? *Even if she did start it.*

"If I were to ask you to do something for me, would you do so?" she asked, pressing her palms to his chest.

His skin heated where she touched, and he drew a deep breath. "Yes," he whispered. It was the truth. There wasn't much she could ask of him in that moment that he would decline. He realized that somehow she managed a hold that no one, save the ones related to him, had over him.

Her soft voice whispered to him in the moonlit library. "Will you touch me?"

CHAPTER EIGHT

Lydia

LYDIA WASN'T SURE when she worked up the nerve to make such a bold request. Her body had been on fire the entire day after their kiss. She had avoided him as much as she could throughout the afternoon and evening, hoping that putting distance between them would ease the intensity of her desire.

When she lay in her bed that evening, all she could think about was how she wanted him to kiss her again and so much more. Even if she knew he was a rake and she would wind up with a broken heart once she allowed herself to do and feel more toward him.

She stared at the canopy and felt the place between her legs ache with need. No matter how many times she tossed and turned, she couldn't get the urge to subside. After that, she took to pacing her chamber, hoping that the activity might tire her out enough to sleep.

That hadn't worked, so she had the idea to select a book, hoping that reading might help her sleep. What she hadn't expected was for the very man, and the object of her intense desire, to appear in the library. Nor had she expected the pull to be so great that she would throw herself at him.

"Miss Cary?" The way he responded to her request was more of a question, and even in the barely lit room, she could see the confusion marring his expression.

"Lydia," she said, drawing another breath. "Will you do as I asked?"

"I'm not certain I know what you mean, Lydia."

She squared her shoulders and raised her chin. She had already gone that far, and there was no turning back now. Either he would give her what she desperately wanted and she could put the urge behind her, or he wouldn't and she'd avoid him for the rest of the house party.

"Elias," she said, enjoying the intimacy of using his given name. She stepped forward and grabbed his hand, pressing it against where she had fantasized about him touching. "Will you touch me here?"

He gulped, and it made her want to kiss his throat.

"You don't know what you ask."

She nodded, noting he hadn't pulled his hand away. "I do."

"But—" he started, before she cut him off.

"I expect nothing from you, and no one ever has to know."

She saw how he warred with himself, which surprised her. Given his status as a known rake, she half expected him to throw her onto the settee and maul her with far less of an invitation. His reaction cracked open a bit of her heart to him, which would be disastrous, so she forced herself to push such thoughts aside.

"Are you not a virgin?" he asked, without a hint of judgment in his tone, but he shifted his hand to grip her hip.

"I am," Lydia said quickly. "What I mean to say is that no man has ever entered me with his…" She trailed off, assuming he knew what she meant. Her mama hadn't been one to leave her daughter in the dark about what occurred between a man and a woman. She hadn't wanted Lydia to go into marriage unaware of such things, but part of her wondered if she wouldn't have allowed certain liberties if she had been less informed. But it was far too late for that.

"But a man has touched you?" His tone had a bit of a jealous edge, which made her heart race.

"Once," she whispered. "Well, kind of, and I'd very much like for you to erase that memory and give me a far better one."

He brought his free hand to her other hip, holding her in place in front of him. "Who touched you? Did he force himself on you? I will ensure he pays for such an offense."

His protective nature only made the place between her legs heat and throb harder, dampening the skin between her thighs. "Nothing like that. And it doesn't matter," she wrapped her arms around his neck. "Please, Elias. I want your touch."

His lips came crashing down on hers in response. She immediately opened to him and took control of the kiss, enjoying the way he growled when she sucked his tongue.

He swept her into his arms as if she were light as a feather, and carried her to the settee, where he laid her down, breaking their kiss.

Standing over her, he untied her dressing robe and opened it so that her night rail was exposed to him. He pulled at the ribbon that tied her hair in place and ran his fingers through her plait, so her hair was loose, splayed out beside her on the cushion.

"So beautiful," he whispered.

His words went straight to her heart, and her chest rose and fell faster from how she fought to steady her breath.

Elias gripped the hem of her night rail and lifted it just slightly, the night air already hitting her thighs, before he paused. "Are you certain this is what you want?"

"More than anything," she whispered.

He groaned and lifted her night rail the rest of the way so that the front laid across her stomach. He placed a single knee on the cushion between her legs, leaving one foot standing on the floor, and then placed a hand by her head to support himself to hover over her.

Using his free hand, he cupped her breast as he brought his lips back to hers. He pulled the top of her night rail down so that both breasts were exposed and hung over the fabric. Kissing down her neck, his tongue ran along the top of her right breast before he sucked the bud of her nipple into his mouth. Lydia arched her back in response, moaning.

He lifted his head to look at her. "Did he do that?"

She shook her head. "No." She said the word so softly she wasn't even certain if he heard her.

"Good." He lowered his head again and did the same thing to her left breast. She grasped his head, holding him there as he licked and sucked.

When he slid his hand further down her body and started massaging her thigh with his hand, she gasped. He hadn't even touched her core yet, and her entire body was on fire wanting him.

Elias shifted his mouth back to meet hers and brushed his fingers over her slit. He began circling the sensitive place that throbbed while he mimicked the movement with his tongue against hers. His fingers slipped lower into her folds until she felt his finger at her opening.

"You have no idea what it does to me to touch you," he said against her lips, then slid his finger inside of her. "You feel so good."

She moaned, and he moved his finger within her. When he slid his finger all the way out, she sank deeper into the settee, prepared to beg him not to stop, but then he must have entered her with two of his fingers given how much more intensely she felt them inside of her when he moved.

"Do you like that?" he whispered.

"Yes," she moaned.

He used his thumb to circle that sensitive place again while he worked his fingers, eliciting from her a stream of moans and whimpers.

"How about that?" he said, but given his amused tone, she didn't believe he expected her to answer.

Besides, she was losing the ability for coherent thought. His touch was far better than anything she had expected, or what it had been her first time.

Elias didn't relent and increased the speed of his movement. "Come on my fingers, Beautiful."

She panted and moaned, and he captured her mouth again to stifle the sounds.

Pulling his head back, she felt the heat of his breath, but her eyes were shut tight.

"Look at me," he commanded.

She blinked her eyes open, and his face was in front of hers, so they were almost nose to nose.

"That's it. Good girl," he whispered. "Eyes on me."

The light from the moon cast shadows on his masculine face, but the intensity in his eyes held her.

"Don't you dare close them when you come, Beautiful."

He applied a bit more pressure with his thumb and it shoved her hard over the edge of bliss. She bucked beneath him, and it took everything in her to keep her eyes trained on his, while she experienced a more intense climax than she had even realized was possible.

It came in wave after wave, over more than several seconds. When the last bit of pleasure reached the tips of her fingers, her body stilled and she fought to catch her breath.

She felt him slowly withdraw his fingers and then he shocked her when he brought them up to his lips and sucked them into his mouth, not taking his eyes off of hers.

He pulled his fingers from his mouth, licking them as he did so. "Mmm. Tastes sweet."

She whimpered at his words, and he lowered his lips to hers again, sweeping his tongue into her mouth, tasting something unfamiliar on his tongue. He kissed her for several moments and then raised his head.

"Is that what you wanted?" he asked, lowering her night rail to cover her legs again.

"And more," she replied, opting for honesty after all that had occurred between them. "Is there something I can do for you? Like touch your…" She would have never felt comfortable offering such a thing to the man she almost married, yet Elias made her feel safe, and if she were honest, even more wanton.

He came to a stand, and she could see the frown forming on his face. "Did this man require you to touch him?"

"No. Never," she said quickly, sensing the jealousy in his tone.

In hindsight, given how she'd never trusted the man, she must have known the entire time that the bounder wasn't the husband for her. But then she caught him with a maid's head between his legs and didn't have to give the matter a second thought.

His expression softened. "This was about giving you pleasure, Beautiful," he said, helping her to stand, then pulling her robe closed, and retying her sash for her. "You needn't worry about me."

Her heart sank into her stomach like a rock. He had no need of her or her inexperience when he had a willing widow sleeping in the very house. For a moment, Lydia had allowed herself to forget that Elias already had an arrangement with a woman.

Part of her found it hard to believe that a man who had shown her such tenderness and care could also be such a cad to go climb on top of another woman, especially after he dared to sound jealous of her past. A past which paled in comparison to the one he was so notorious for.

She should have let it go, but the notion irritated and nagged at her insides to the point where she was about to explode. "Elias?"

"Yes? I'm afraid I will be of no use to set your hair to its rights, but I couldn't resist seeing you thus."

She drew a deep breath, at war with what she knew of his reputation and what she had witnessed between him and Lady Billings, compared to how he had been with her this evening. How he called her "Beautiful" and looked at her as if she were precious to him.

It would be far better to know the truth. Besides, she'd go

mad if she didn't ask. "Are you going to leave here and seek Lady Billings's bed?"

He flinched as if she had slapped him. "Of course not. Why would you think that?"

"You have before. Probably last night, even." She didn't bother to hide the hurt she felt. Although she knew he was a rake when she made her request. So she was the only one to blame.

He cupped her cheek, and her heart raced again. "I haven't been with that woman in a few years, and I shall never do so again."

"You don't have to lie to me," she whimpered, tears forming at the corners of her eyes, which she instantly hated herself for. She had no right to react in that way about such things, especially when she told him she expected nothing from him.

"I'm not lying."

"Just stop, Elias," she said, pulling her face from his hand. "I heard you that first night. And besides, I suppose it's none of my business anyhow."

"Lydia," he whispered, stepping closer to her. "You must not have heard the part where I told her I didn't want her. Ever. And that is the truth."

She closed her eyes, allowing him to cup her cheek again. Fool as she was, she believed him. "I'm sorry. I just thought…"

"Please don't apologize. I am well aware of what my reputation is. But I would never have so little respect for you to share what we did and then pursue another woman."

She nodded, her throat thick with emotion. She reminded herself not to lose her heart to him, as nothing would come from what had occurred.

He placed a tender kiss on her lips and then placed her hand in the crook of his arm. "Do you think you can sleep now?" he asked, grinning at her.

She laughed and covered her face with her free hand, embarrassed that he remembered. "Indeed."

"Then I have done my job. Let's get you back upstairs, and

then I shall adjourn to my chamber. Alone, I might add."

He led her out of the library, and they moved cautiously through the corridor and up the stairs, careful not to make a sound. When they reached the top of the stairs, his lips brushed her ear. "Go straight to your chamber. I will remain here in the shadows until I hear your door close."

She kissed his cheek—unsure why she had done so—and then hurried off down the hall, only a couple of doors away, until she swept into her chamber, not attempting to be completely silent when she closed the door so that Elias could hear it.

Lydia tossed herself across her bed with a silly smile lingering on her face. She told herself that when she had dared to ask for what she wanted, it would only be to meet her physical needs. Why couldn't she use him the way he used other women to curb his desires? But there appeared to be much more to him than she realized.

Yawning, she positioned herself with her head on her pillow and threw her covers over herself. She needed her rest, because she already knew that one time experiencing ecstasy with Elias wouldn't be enough. If good sense were a cliff, she had already dived off the edge that evening. She'd have to be much stronger when it came to Elias, if she didn't wish to find herself hurt by another rake.

CHAPTER NINE

Elias

ELIAS WOKE UP the next morning with his cock still just as hard as it had been the night before. As soon as he had heard Lydia's door click closed, he hurried to his own chamber, grinning to himself at the events in the library. He immediately sent his valet to bed for the evening. Before the length of two breaths had passed, he had locked the door and released his cock, which had painfully strained against his falls. He hadn't taken himself in hand like a green lad in quite a long time, but the way he throbbed, he'd never find sleep if he didn't sate his needs.

He had fisted himself where he stood, stroking himself with a jerky, hurried frenzy. After only a few moments, he had soiled his handkerchief. Not attempting to muffle his groans.

By the time he undressed and completed his evening ablutions, his cock was erect again. He widened his stance where he stood and stroked his length again, making slower movements that time. Imagining the taste of Lydia on his fingers and the way her face looked when she came. With his breathing ragged and a few beads of sweat on his brow, he'd released several low moans when he spent his seed in another cloth.

Sighing at the sight of the return of his erect cock from where he lay on his back in his bed, he closed his eyes again. It would be problematic if he couldn't get his body under control, especially once he found himself in Lydia's presence again. Even a brush of her body against his might be enough to make him spend.

He had been in a state of shock and disbelief when she made her request to him. Using all of his willpower, he had intended to decline her request, recalling everything his father said and the thoughts he had about his future. But something about her was irresistible, and he was sucked into the center of her web.

Once he had agreed, he promised himself that he wouldn't take any of his own pleasure from her. That was the only way he could feel like he wasn't taking advantage of her—if he made the moment only about Lydia receiving all the attention at that moment.

He sighed again and threw the covers back, deciding to accept his fate. He would fuck his own hand again and hope that it would sate his desire. Laying in his bed, he tightened his muscular legs and tightened his hand around his shaft, replaying the previous evening in his mind with each tight stroke. By the time he came again, shooting streams of his spend across his stomach, the tension diminished from his shoulders.

Another moment of their conversation came to mind. When she'd asked him if he would seek Lady Billings, it stung more than he cared to admit. He had spent so long in his carefree life as a rake that he didn't consider what someone like Lydia might think of his character.

The dratted words of his father hit him again. If he had any doubt that he wanted something different for his life, it was becoming clearer that he no longer wished to be known as a rake. A lifestyle of endless merriment had lost its luster.

The tension returned, but at least his cock remained mostly flaccid. Elias still wasn't convinced that love would have any place in his future. It was one thing to succumb to the life of a respectable gentleman, but it was another matter entirely to give himself over to the notion of love.

Climbing from his bed, he went to the wash basin and cleaned his stomach, then went about washing up to dress for the day. He rang for Flint, his valet, while he set about donning a pair of breeches.

While Flint helped him dress for the day, he pondered what reaction Lydia would have to him at breakfast. Although, he must remember to refer to her as Miss Cary in front of the rest of the guests, given that he'd become far too accustomed to thinking of her by her given name. His sisters would attack him with questions and suspicions if he slipped.

He only hoped she wouldn't feel embarrassed about what had occurred between them. If he were honest, he looked forward to seeing her, and he hoped she might also be glad to see him. But he wouldn't allow himself to think more about why he felt that way. He had decided that he would spend the day getting to know her better. Perhaps he might even learn why she had propositioned him the way she had. He could admit that he was more than curious. It wasn't every day that an innocent unmarried miss made such a request.

Once he was dressed and looked the part of the noble viscount, he departed his chamber and made his way to the breakfast room, hearing the low roar of conversation before he even crossed the threshold.

He immediately saw Lydia—Miss Cary, he reminded himself—sitting with his sisters again. After he made his selections from the sideboard, he took the available seat between Miss Cary and his father. "Good morning, everyone," he said cheerily, then turned to Lydia. "You as well, Miss Cary." He flashed her a wide smile, and her cheeks turned a faint pink.

Her reaction did nothing to aid in his need to keep his body under control. He imagined, with only the whisper of a few words, he could turn those cheeks from pink to red. Then he reminded himself he didn't want to be known as a rake anymore. Although, a bit of flirting and naughty words would be among the lesser of sins he had committed in the past.

"Good morning, my lord," she said, then bit off a piece of her toast.

His family all cast him a curious glance, and he schooled his features so his family wouldn't find his pleasant mood—at being in the presence of the delectable Miss Cary—something to suspect.

"Sleep well, son?" his father asked him, and Elias had a feeling he was actually asking a different question.

"I slept fine," Elias said, spearing a bite of egg and bringing it to his mouth.

"Are you going to continue to disappear in the middle of the night?" Diana asked him.

He rolled his eyes. "We just went out for a bit. And, no, I believe we shall be at your mercy for the duration of the events, sister."

"Good," she said. "And I expect you and the other men to each escort one of the ladies to the village today."

"Of course," he said, giving his sister a small nod. Realizing that the trip would create the perfect opportunity to learn more about Lydia. "Miss Cary, might I escort you today?"

She glanced at him as if she might decline his request, and his smile faded.

But then she cooly replied, "I would enjoy your company, my lord. Thank you." Her tone was proper and gave no inclination at what she might be thinking.

Elias turned back to meet his sister's gaze. "I will ensure the rest of the gents play the part of the dutiful escorts."

"Thank you, brother," Diana said. "I believe I shall ask Jude to be my escort."

He narrowed his eyes on Diana. "You aren't developing a tendre for him, are you, sister? He shall never marry. You've known him since you were a girl barely out of her leading strings."

Diana huffed and rolled her eyes. "No, brother. I don't harbor any feelings for Jude. He is merely entertaining company."

"How entertaining?" Elias asked, glancing down the table as Jude grinned at something another guest had said, the dimples that earned him unrelenting attention from countless women on full display. He wouldn't typically suspect one of his closest friends of dallying with his sister. But after Elias had pleasured an innocent in his family's home last night, who knew what temptation might cause someone to do?

"Elias, you are being ridiculous," Diana hissed. "Jude would never. Nor would I wish for him to."

Elias drew a deep breath. "He can be quite scandalous, Diana. And one can't be too cautious in matters of their sister's honor."

"I suppose you are the expert on scandalous behavior," she said, her nostrils flaring.

He cast a sideways glance at Lydia, who sat with wide eyes, watching the siblings bicker with each other. Giggles from Jenny and Grace broke through the brief silence at the table.

"That's enough. Both of you," their father said, then turned toward Elias. "I trust Jude, Matt, and Hudson almost the same as I trust you, Elias, to keep your sisters safe." He paused and turned his head to capture Diana's gaze. "And Diana, don't be unkind to your brother for caring about your well-being. I depend on him to do so." His father glanced at Lydia for a moment—which Elias found curious—and then back to Diana. "Give your brother room to learn and find his way."

Elias was irritated that Lydia witnessed their scolding, or perhaps it was embarrassment. His father announced to the lot of them that Elias needed to grow up, even if he hadn't said those exact words.

He'd take the high road to salvage the situation. "You are right, Father," Elias said. "My apologies, sister." It was still hard for him to accept that the annoying little sister who used to beg to follow him around was old enough to take a husband and start a family of her own.

She nodded at him. "I also apologize, brother."

The rest of breakfast passed by with more pleasant conversation. Jenny and Grace asked Diana to bring back a bit of red ribbon to wear in their hair on Christmas Eve, and they spoke of some treats they hoped Cook would prepare. Elias had no doubt that Diana would already have things well in hand and everyone's favorites would be prepared for them. Just as his mother would have done.

He glanced at Lydia again. She had said little during the entire breakfast, but he supposed it was hard to get a word in with his family.

Diana encouraged the guests to pair off and line up to await the carriages. Matt attempted to accompany Hannah, but Hudson quickly stepped between them and stated that he would escort his sister. Hudson really could hold a grudge. They all knew the ill will between the men had nothing to do with Hannah since their falling out occurred while they were all at university, but Hudson didn't appear to want his sister to be friends with Matt, either.

The first carriage arrived, and Elias handed Lydia up the steps and then entered to sit beside her. Then Hudson handed Hannah up to join them and they took their seats across from Elias and Lydia.

"Matt would do nothing untoward to Hannah," Elias said, catching Hudson's stare, which was more of an annoyed frown.

"Who knows what the bounder is capable of," Hudson snarled.

Elias laughed. "This is Matt we are talking about. The most upstanding of us all. Just tell me what happened so we can put it to rest. I beg you, Hudson."

"Please," Hannah begged from beside him, a disdainful edge to her tone.

"Drop it," Hudson ground out. "Get it through your thick skull that I shall never speak of it. Let's not ruin our holiday over Wilton."

Elias rolled his eyes. He could argue that it was Hudson who would ruin the merry mood, but when Hudson dug his heels in, he couldn't be moved. Elias decided he'd never ask him about it again.

"Miss Cary," Elias said, shifting his focus to Lydia, "is there something you are looking for while we are in the village?"

Of the questions he might have for the lady, that one was at the bottom of the list, but one of the few he could ask in front of Hudson and Hannah.

"I'm uncertain," she replied, maintaining her state of indifference toward him. "I'd just like to browse the shops."

The rest of the brief carriage ride passed in silence. Once the carriage stopped, Elias jumped up to help Lydia down first, hoping they could distance themselves from Hudson and Hannah. Instead of handing her down, he grabbed her by her waist and lifted her to the ground.

Her breath caught from the action, and he was relieved to see that his touch still affected her. He set her down in front of him, and quickly tucked her hand in the crook of his arm, before leading her away.

"We are going this way," he called over his shoulder to Hudson, hoping his friend would take the hint.

"My lord," Lydia said, once they were on their own walking down the street. "You needn't accompany me out of some misguided honor. I told you I expect nothing from you."

"I...I didn't think you did," he replied. "I want to spend time with you, as I would like to get to know you better." She was all he had been thinking about, which could prove problematic. But he wouldn't speak those words.

She laughed. "We both know you are a rake, Lord Snowdon. Even your sister knows so. While you aren't completely without honor, or you would have taken more liberties and likely avoided my company today, but you are still a rake. You are free to go about your life and leave me to mine."

"I am Elias to you," he ground out. Her words struck him with a painful blow. "And perhaps I wish to change. How can I do so if you, and the rest of the world, refuse to see me any other way?" He wasn't certain why he had allowed himself to speak those words and had to fight to keep from looking away from her in his embarrassment.

Elias watched her expression shift from a hard stare to one of remorse. "You are right," she sighed, contemplating him. "Perhaps you deserve an opportunity to prove yourself. It isn't easy for me to trust, but if what you say is true, in the spirit of the Christmas season, I shall give you a chance to prove yourself and will spend the day with you."

They walked in silence for a few moments, but Elias couldn't let go of the comment she made.

"Why are you unable to trust? Is it because of the man you won't tell me about?" He would bet a small fortune on that being the case. "You should know that you can tell me anything," he said softly.

"Yes," she said, her voice almost a whisper. "It is because of him."

"I know it's forward of me to ask, but given that..." he paused and glanced around them. "Well, you know...I think such things might be forgiven. Will you tell me what happened?"

She shrugged. "It wasn't much unlike what happens all the time in our society. I thought myself to be, well, not in love if I am honest, but to have some kind of affection for the man. He proposed, and I accepted, believing the match to be better than most would be afforded. He was full of wicked words and promises." Lydia drew a deep breath. "And I allowed him to take some liberties."

Elias's jaw clenched tighter at every word she spoke, but he forced himself to remain quiet and allow her to finish speaking.

"I snuck out of my family's London townhouse one day to venture to his home. When I arrived, I found him enjoying the attention of a maid on her knees in front of him. When he saw me in the doorway, he didn't even tell her to stop and just expected that I should accept the future for what it would be."

"The bastard," Elias seethed. He might have been guilty of a libertine lifestyle, but he would never do something so disrespectful and horrid. To any woman.

"My father handled the matter, and all remained hidden,

although I understand that the man was quite angry over my crying off from the betrothal. It would seem my dowry would have proved beneficial to him to resolve some of his debts."

"You deserve far better than that, Lydia," he said, tamping down his anger. "I hope you know the fault lies with him and not with you."

She nodded. "I didn't at first, but I do now."

"Tell me who he is."

Lydia shook her head. "Nothing good can come from it. The matter is dead and buried and I don't need saving, Elias."

He stopped walking and turned her to face him. "Please tell me. If I know who he is, I can protect you if he should dare to speak to you."

She contemplated him, then opened her mouth and closed it again.

"Lydia, you can trust me."

Lydia released a long breath. "It was Clint. Errr...Lord Durham."

Hell and damnation. If he had known, he would have planted the man several facers at the tavern. Durham deserved far worse.

"Thank you for telling me. I will do everything in my power to ensure you never have to be in the same room with him again."

Elias knew the blackguard had reacted oddly when they had shared the attendees of the house party. After the holiday and Lydia was safely on her way home, Elias would make a brief trip to Downe's home where Durham was staying and ensure that he knew what would happen to him if he dared to cross Lydia's path.

Elias hadn't felt such a powerful urge to protect anyone other than his sisters, and his reaction to the poor treatment that Lydia had suffered rivaled that. The anger and fierce need to see to her well-being gave him far more questions than answers.

Suddenly, the hairs on the back of his neck stood up, and he had a nagging feeling like someone was watching them. He glanced around and didn't see anyone. Nor did he notice anything suspicious. Narrowing his eyes, he scanned the area once more.

Looking back at Lydia, he shook off the concern. The innocent way she licked her bottom lip shifted his thoughts to the previous evening when he'd made her breathless from his hand.

He wasn't certain he wished to know the answer to his next question, but he had to ask. "Did you ask what you did of me in the library because you thought me to be a rake who had fortuitously appeared to you, or for some other reason?"

She gulped and searched his face as if she were looking for something. "I…well, if someone else had been the one to enter the library, I wouldn't have asked the same of them. If that is what you are asking."

His heart beat so hard in his chest, he thought she might hear it. "That's part of it. But did you proposition me because you believed me to be a rake who would give you what you wanted, or because you wanted me?"

Lydia shook her head. "Please don't make me answer that."

He glanced around them, and then pulled them into an alley where they had a better chance of going unseen. Turning her to face him again, he lightly clasped her shoulders. "I need to know."

"I did believe you to be a rake," she started, shifting on her feet. "But that wasn't why," she whispered, looking up at him through her lashes, her eyes pleading with him to understand her meaning. Her cheeks turned a deep crimson, and she was irresistible.

The sight knocked the wind from his body. He drew a deep breath and then stepped forward, pressing her back against the brick wall as he lowered his lips to hers. She opened for him immediately, and their tongues collided.

Elias warred with his body as his hands found her hips and pulled the bottom half of her against him. She gripped his hair and held his mouth against hers as she took more control over the kiss. The bulge of his cock throbbed against her, aching for even the lightest of touch.

Remembering where they were, and that she was still an

innocent—albeit not entirely so—he forced himself to break the kiss. He was supposed to be leaving his rakish behavior behind.

"We risk being seen," he whispered.

She nodded, her lips pink and swollen. He wanted to press her back against the wall and kiss her again, but the last remaining bit of his good sense urged him to do otherwise. His thoughts weren't completely reformed, as he could imagine turning her around to face the coarse brick, lifting her skirts, and making quick work of pleasing them both. The fleeting daydream did nothing to settle his cock.

Poking his head out, he made sure no one was looking and then pulled her back onto the street. They began walking again, her hand gripping his arm.

The electricity from her touch continued to do things to him, and it became far too difficult for him to ignore or brush off as nothing.

Before he could ponder further, his body tensed again as if he felt eyes on them. He turned and noticed Lady Billings exiting a shop on the other side of the street, then heading in the opposite direction from where he and Lydia faced.

He didn't believe Lady Billings saw what he and Lydia had done, especially if she was inside the shop, but could she have been watching them earlier when they were on the street? Elias shook off the concern, determining it was nothing, and that he was just being overly cautious. Instead, he refocused all of his attention on Lydia, and the fear that she was becoming far too important to him.

Elias wondered if what he felt had been what his father tried to describe. He did his best to shake that off too. Everything he believed he knew was changing far too fast, and he wasn't certain he was ready to accept it. But the thought of Lydia leaving him at the end of the house party wasn't something he was ready for, either. And that notion terrified him most of all.

CHAPTER TEN

Lydia

LYDIA WOKE UP the morning of Christmas Eve still tense with need after she and Elias kissed in the alley the day before. She was starting to admit to herself that it wasn't just for his handsome appearance, although there wasn't a more handsome man alive in her opinion. He differed from what she thought he would be. He had proven himself to be protective and considerate, even caring.

When he expressed his desire to change from his rakish reputation, she had allowed herself to hope. Hope for what? She wasn't certain. He made her feel things that no other man had, and it was just as thrilling as it was frightening.

The previous evening, when everyone played various games in the drawing room, she lost her ability to think every time his sandalwood scent invaded her senses. She had every urge to pull him from the room and beg him to do much more than what they shared previously.

Based on his reaction to her and the heat in his expression when he caught her gaze, she believed he had similar urges, but to his dratted credit, he remained the picture of a gentleman. She supposed she was the wicked one, desiring to corrupt the man who longed to abandon his rakish lifestyle. Although, he didn't need to reform himself completely, did he?

After Tilly helped Lydia dress for the day, she joined the rest of the guests for breakfast, deciding she didn't wish to wait for her parents. Once she had made her selections at the sideboard, she took one of the open seats across from Elias's sisters, as she had for the last few mornings. She found she adored the sisters very much, even their arguing and banter. As an only child, she would have enjoyed having sisters to grow up with.

Not long after Lydia sat down, Hannah took the seat on Lydia's right. The seat on her left remained open, and she could admit that she hoped Elias would be the one to sit there.

"Are we decorating today?" Hannah asked, her attention focused on Diana.

"Indeed. I planned to send everyone out to collect the greenery and the yule log after we break our fast," Diana replied, then took a bite of her toast.

Lydia recalled the last time she had traipsed through the woods with Elias. She might have to encourage him to take her to that very spot. They would need to gather mistletoe for the kissing balls anyway, and fortunately, she and Elias knew exactly where to find some.

She licked her lips at the memory, and then her body tingled from awareness. The chair beside her moved, and she knew it was him before he sat down, almost as if she had conjured him from her thoughts.

"You look beautiful today, Miss Cary," he said, using her more formal address in front of his sisters. She understood, but she far preferred the intimacy of him using her given name.

"Thank you, my lord," she replied, casting him a sideways glance and grinning.

Grace huffed from across the table. "You said nothing about how we look today, brother."

Lydia brought her napkin to her lips to hide her laughter.

"You look lovely today, sisters," he said, waving to all of them. "You too, Hannah. Can't have you chastising me for leaving you out as well."

"There are far better things to chastise you about, Elias," Hannah replied, shaking her head.

Lydia tamped down her irritation. How was it acceptable for him to be on familiar terms with Hannah, but he had to be so formal with Lydia? She thought he might have felt something more for her after yesterday, but if he was still keeping her at a distance with his family, was that not the case?

A more troubling thought came to her mind. Had he already experienced stolen kisses, or other things, with Hannah? He said he wanted to change, but the man was a rake. He had an unknown number of partners he'd met for trysts.

Lydia sat through breakfast, hardly hearing anything that anyone said. The sisters were arguing about something, and they pulled Elias into the banter. She couldn't focus on what it had been about, as she was too busy thinking about how many women the man beside her had dallied with. How many of them cared about him and then had their hearts broken? Lydia was almost certain that she was halfway on the path to allowing herself to love him, as foolish as she was, since the odds weighed heavier on her leaving the Snowdon estate with a broken heart.

After breakfast, Diana urged them all outside with baskets and cutters, with instructions on what greenery to collect so that they could all decorate the house to prepare for Christmas. They would have a grand celebration that evening with dinner and carols, and then continue the merriment the next day.

Deciding it might be best to take off alone to ponder more of her thoughts, Lydia took a basket and started off toward the trees. She only just got to the tree line when Elias appeared beside her, huffing.

"I thought we might work together," he said, grabbing her wrist to stop her. And she believed he also did so to allow himself a chance to catch his breath.

"How many other ladies present have you 'worked' with, my lord?" She knew she sounded like a petulant child, or at best a nagging wife, with her tone, and regretted it as soon as she spoke the words. Besides, wasn't she the one who told him she expected nothing from him? But that was before she had allowed herself to feel something for him.

Confusion marred his expression. "You already know about Lady Billings. And that is long done. I promise you."

"Who else don't I know about?" She just couldn't leave well enough alone. She had to know.

"I don't know what you mean, Lydia."

She pulled her wrist from his hand and hurried away from him into the woods. Even though she knew she was being ridiculous and she had no right to feel the way she did, she was too overcome with jealousy to maintain rational thought.

He made quick work of catching up with her, grabbing her wrist again and spinning her to face him. "Please stop running away from me," he said with no anger in his tone.

She searched his expression and found nothing but tenderness there. Her chest rose and fell, as all that she could hear over her ragged breath was the distant crunching of snow where other guests had trudged in the opposite direction of where they had gone.

"Lydia," he started again, "tell me what it is you wish to know."

She glanced to her feet, trying to summon the words.

"Eyes on me, Beautiful," he whispered.

Lydia looked up at him, the urge to kiss him far too great. She drew a long breath. "Have you kissed or been intimate with any of the other ladies who are here?"

"No," he answered quickly, not removing his gaze from hers. "Not a single one."

She released a sigh of relief.

"Is that what upsets you?" he asked. "You believed me to dally with the other young ladies?" He dramatically put his hand over his heart. "You wound me if you think so."

Reaching for his hand, she shook her head. "I'm sorry. I just…you were so familiar with Hannah. It got me thinking. I…I don't know who all you have been with. It could be anyone I am acquainted with."

He squeezed her hand tighter. "Hannah is practically my sister. I've known her since she and Diana were tiny girls following Hudson and me all over these estates," he said, drawing a deep breath. "I can't change my past. But," he paused and gulped, "for you, I aim to be a better man. I am done with that part of my life, and I only wish to move forward."

She gasped, unsure if she understood his meaning. Did his words mean he intended to move forward with her?

Before she could ask, he had pulled her against him and softly pressed his lips to hers. The kiss was so tender and sweet, it almost brought tears to her eyes. She sank into him, and deepened their kiss, somehow feeling like something had shifted between them. Something that told her she knew she had already lost her heart to Elias.

There was no use in trying to fight it any longer. She was in love with Viscount Snowdon, and her heart soared. She wasn't sure how she'd speak the words to him, or when he might be ready to hear them, but she hoped that one day he just might feel the same.

He walked her back, so that she was pressed up against a tree and his kiss turned into one of need. Elias feathered kisses along her jaw, and lightly nibbled at her neck before soothing the bite with his tongue.

"I want you, Elias," she whispered. Not exactly the same as professing the depths of her love for him, but still also a highly accurate statement.

He growled against her neck. "You are a temptress, Beautiful."

"Please," she said, pressing her hips tighter against him. All the need from the day prior and how she lay in bed thinking of him and wishing that he would sneak into her room and touch her as he had before came flooding back and consumed her. She had a never-ending ache, and only he could provide the release she so desperately wanted.

Elias picked up his head and glanced around. They had been fortunate not to have anyone come across them, thanks to a thick patch of trees that had shielded them.

"Come with me," he said, grabbing her hand and pulling her with him.

"Where are we going?" she asked, watching her steps to ensure she didn't trip.

"We have a hunting cabin just this way."

The place between her thighs heated, anticipating that soon she would be nothing but a moaning wanton in his arms. Or hoping, rather. Definitely hoping.

They moved through the woods for what seemed like ten minutes or so until the cabin came into view. Once they reached it, he ushered her inside.

She grabbed for him to kiss him again, but he stepped back. "Allow me to start a fire, first," he said. "I don't want you catching a chill."

"A fire would be nice." She watched him arrange logs in the fireplace. The cabin appeared to have two rooms, one that was a sleeping chamber and the rest was a large, open area.

A few minutes later, he had the flame started, and it didn't take long before the fire roared to life and began heating the room.

Elias stepped back over to her. "I couldn't remove your pelisse without ensuring you would be warm enough," he said as he unbuttoned the pelisse and pushed it off her shoulders. He laid it across a nearby chair, then removed his greatcoat and placed it on top.

"That's better," he said, cupping her cheek and lowering his lips to hers.

She responded by clasping her hands behind his neck, holding him in place when she opened to him and met his tongue with hers. She tasted his tea from breakfast as she explored his mouth, pressing herself tighter against him.

A hard bulge between his legs pressed against her stomach. She had never seen what lay beneath a man's breeches, aside from the statues on display at the museum. Even when she walked in on Durham, she couldn't see him since his maid's head blocked her view.

Lydia pushed all thoughts of the blackguard out of her mind, only caring for and desiring the man before her. She found she longed to please him. To know what he enjoyed and to be the one to satisfy all of his needs.

Continuing to kiss him, she moved one of her hands slowly down his body, continuing until she reached the bulge, cupping it in her hand and giving it a gentle squeeze.

Elias broke the kiss, panting to catch his breath. "What are you doing?"

"I want to touch you." She rubbed, and his member felt hard as a rock beneath the fabric.

He clasped her hand. "I don't want to take advantage of you, and we haven't yet discussed what we are to each other."

Lydia removed her other hand from behind his neck and shifted it between them to unfasten his falls. "You aren't taking advantage. I want this, Elias. Please."

He didn't stop her and closed his eyes when she used both hands to unbutton the fabric the rest of the way until his thick shaft protruded between them. Lydia ran her fingers along the smooth skin, and he sucked in a breath of air.

"Eyes on me, Handsome," she teased him. She wasn't certain where her boldness came from. It could only be from how much she wanted him, and how safe and comfortable she felt in his presence. He wouldn't do a single thing she didn't wish to do, and that made her more daring and bold.

Elias opened his eyes and the heat that shone in them made that place between her thighs ache. She tightened her hand around his shaft and explored his length, noting his breath became more ragged when she stroked him.

"You're going to make me spend," he groaned breathily.

"Good," she said, looking down at his cock, which had a bit of liquid on the tip. She brushed over it with the thumb of her other hand. Bringing it to her mouth, she sucked her thumb between her lips, catching his gaze when she did so, just as he had done to the fingers that he'd had inside of her.

The taste was just a bit salty, and she felt the most powerful she'd ever been in her life, bringing pleasure to a man. Particularly this man.

He growled and walked her back until the back of her legs were against the settee, and he urged her to sit. She was eye level with his cock, and her immediate thought was that she wanted to take all of him into her mouth, but before she could move, he knelt to the floor.

Elias lifted her skirts, and the warm heat from the fire kissed her skin. He gripped her knees and spread her legs apart, settling himself between them.

"Elias," she whispered.

"I'm going to lick and taste you until you come on my tongue, and then if you have energy left, you can do whatever you wish to me."

She whimpered at his words and she fought to keep her eyes on him, knowing he would tell her to do so if she closed them.

He gripped her bottom and scooted her to the edge of the cushion, then urged her to lean back against the backrest. She felt his tongue run along the slit of her folds until it reached the place that made her buck and moan.

Elias picked his head up, and as wanton as she was, she hated that he had stopped.

"Place your legs over my shoulders," he said.

She did as he said, her stockinged legs resting on his back. They hadn't even bothered to remove their shoes. He placed each of his hands on the inside of her thighs and spread her legs apart.

When he resumed licking her, she released a loud stream of moans. He slid a finger inside of her core and raised his head again, watching her move against his hand.

"That's it, Beautiful," he said. "You can be as loud as you want. Show me how much you enjoy what I'm doing to you."

"Elias," she moaned, rocking her hips on his fingers when he added a second one.

"Yes. Just like that," he said, smirking at her before he lowered his head again.

He removed his fingers, and then she felt his tongue enter her. How had she never known that mouths could bring so much pleasure? It was wanton and wicked, but she tightened her thighs on his head and moved against his face, urging his tongue to enter her as deep as he could.

Elias pressed his thumb against the opening to her slit and circled it while he continued to move his tongue inside of her. When he did so, she lost all rational thought. She moaned and cried out with abandon, arching her back from the intensity of the ecstasy between her thighs.

She imagined what his cock would feel like in place of his tongue, and what his naked, warm, muscular body would feel like pressed against hers.

When she couldn't hold out any longer, her toes curled, and she stilled, almost yelling his name as the waves of her climax hummed throughout her entire body for several seconds. Nothing had ever felt better in her life, almost as if she were flying through the sky. She wasn't certain she would survive if they were to couple, as the blissful state he would put her in would be far too much for her body to handle.

When she went limp and sank back into the settee, she moaned again from the sensation of him continuing to work his tongue inside of her, growling to himself as he did so.

Finally, he picked his head up and caught her gaze. "I couldn't let any of you go to waste."

Her skin heated from his words, and she leaned forward and clasped his lapels to pull him toward her. When she kissed him, the taste of herself on him made her long to give in to her wicked desires, even more so than she had before. She pulled back and pressed her forehead to his. "My handsome lord, I believe I was promised a turn."

"You really don't have to, Lydia," he said, but his tone indicated he didn't exactly wish to dissuade her from the notion completely.

"I want to, Elias."

His cock jutted out from where he was positioned on his knees, and he stroked his length with his right hand. She loved watching him do so and wondered if what he felt was the same as what it had been for her.

"What is it you have a mind to do, Beautiful?"

"Come to your feet, and I shall show you," she said, her boldness returning at the realization that she would control what he felt. That she could do to him what he did to her, and drive him to the same brink of madness.

Elias slowly stood and looked down at her with only the slightest hesitation. She looked up at him and grinned, taking his cock into her hand to stroke it.

"I want to taste you," she said, biting into her bottom lip. "Will you tell me what to do?"

His cock twitched in her hand. "Just take a little into your mouth at a time until you are comfortable, sucking and licking as you move your mouth as you do your hand," he said slowly and between quick breaths.

She ran her tongue over the tip of his cock, and looked up at him, finding him staring back at her, his eyes almost black with desire.

"That's a good girl," he whispered. "You didn't even make me remind you to keep your eyes on mine."

She kept her eyes fixed on his as she sucked more of him into her mouth, licking along the bottom of his cock until she couldn't take him in any further. She sucked and licked with him deep in her mouth and his hands shot to her head, sinking his fingers into her hair.

"So, good, Beautiful," he moaned.

Lydia responded by sucking hard and moving her mouth back and forth on his length. Each time she sucked him back into her mouth, he gripped her head tighter.

When he let his head roll back, she sucked him faster, believing that doing so would push him over the same cliff that he had brought her to.

He moaned and rocked his hips with her movements, helping her to take him deeper into her mouth.

"Lydia," he moaned, almost in a panic. "I'm going to…you must stop…or I'll…I'm going to spend."

There was no way she was going to stop. She would taste him the same way he'd done with her. She gripped the back of his thighs and looked back up at him as she worked her tongue harder against his shaft.

He groaned and moaned her name several times as her mouth filled with something thick and warm. She swallowed it down, and he cupped her cheek as he stared into her eyes. After several seconds, he collapsed beside her on the settee.

Lydia watched him as he tucked himself back inside his breeches, and she righted her skirts. He pulled her against him to settle into his side with his arm around her.

Elias kissed her temple. "You are wonderful," he whispered. "Nothing has ever felt better."

"I quite agree," she said, nuzzling against his clothed chest. She realized she still hadn't seen him with no clothing, but based on how firm his chest was, she imagined he would be delightful to gaze upon.

"I wish for us to speak about what the future could hold for us, but not now," he said. "Not directly after I was a cad who spent in your wicked mouth."

She pulled back and smirked at him. "I made you do so."

"That you did, Beautiful," he said, sighing. "But some things must be handled properly, but just know that I wish to speak with you on the matter."

Lydia fought to hide her excitement. Surely if he meant to

speak with her, he would ask for her hand. He would need Papa's permission, of course, which is why he needed to wait. Although, a small part of her worried that he only did so because of what occurred and not for a strong affection for her. He had yet to speak the words. But she reminded herself that he'd been nothing but caring and considerate to her, which would mean he couldn't be completely devoid of feelings.

They remained silent for a few moments, with her leaning against his chest and Elias lazily rubbing her back, both staring at the fire. She imagined the same scene playing out for years to come. She imagined Christmases before the fire with their children, already knowing that he'd make the most devoted father.

"We really should get back," he said, breaking the silence. "We shall need to cut some greenery and mistletoe on our way or they'll surely question why we have been gone so long and have returned with an empty basket."

She laughed. "At least we already know where to find mistletoe. Assuming we don't dally when we find it."

CHAPTER ELEVEN

Elias

ELIAS CHASTISED HIMSELF for allowing an innocent to wrap her sweet lips around his cock. Even if it had been the most thrilling experience of his life. But he was trying to be less of a rake, and the first time he got her alone again, he had his head between her legs and pulled his cock out.

He had already decided he was going to offer for her, having realized that they would suit perfectly for a contented marriage. There wasn't a single other person whose company he had enjoyed more, and they were obviously quite compatible when it came to the more physical aspects of a marriage.

A strong marriage could be built on those things, even if love wouldn't play a part in their future. He'd appreciate her and value her, but love was the only thing he couldn't give her. Or wouldn't give her, rather. Surely she would be content if she had every-thing else from him. He'd honor their marriage vows and remain faithful to her. After the time they had spent together over the last few days, even if it was fast, there wasn't a doubt in his mind that he wouldn't want another woman.

If he could allow himself to love any woman and give her his whole heart, it would be Lydia. Perhaps that is how he could explain things, and she'd understand.

She never said she wanted a love match and admitted she

hadn't loved the man she had been temporarily betrothed to.

Elias groaned to himself at the recollection of Durham. He was still another matter for Elias to handle. As Lydia's husband, Elias would make the man's life miserable if he should dare to speak to her.

He and Lydia were almost back to the house with the bundle of greenery that they had collected. Elias couldn't help himself when they reached the mistletoe and had to pull her in for a kiss or several.

Diana would surely give him her annoying knowing look when they returned, but she wouldn't make a show of it to the other guests. He knew he could count on his sister for that.

When they reached the back of the house, another group of guests were just ahead of them going inside, so at least they weren't too far behind.

Once they were inside, and a servant had taken their outer garments, Elias dropped the basket down beside the others. Diana got everyone to work making kissing balls and stringing garlands together with the greenery so that she could direct the servants where to place them.

Elias settled into a chair beside Lydia and watched her delicate fingers work to craft the decorations.

"You could help, brother," Diana said, waving for him to see how the others were all working. Jenny and Grace were the most excited, since it was one activity they could be present for.

"Come now, sister, you know I am no good at this," he groaned.

"What I know is that you use that excuse every year to get out of helping."

He put his hand over his heart dramatically. "You wound me, sister."

She smirked at him. "But that reminds me. I owe you both a prize. And your prize is that you two get to be the ones to direct the placement of the kissing balls. You can make them as easy or as difficult as you wish for our guests to get caught under them."

While he liked the idea of knowing where we could pull Lydia whenever he wanted, his eyebrow arched. "Is that your clever way of being able to feign ignorance if I catch you beneath one with one of these gents?"

"Still worried I'm after Jude, brother? Perhaps I've tired of him and moved on to Matt now."

Elias pinched the bridge of his nose. "Leave all of my friends alone."

Diana lowered her voice where only he could hear her. "Perhaps it's you who carries the guilt of dallying with one's friend, brother."

"Don't," he ground out.

"Then get it through your thick, bacon-brained skull that your friends are like brothers to me, and that is it."

He was inclined to believe her. She didn't possess her usual telltale signs that she was hiding something, and she had never acted as if she had an interest in any of them. It was hard to stop playing the role of the protective older brother, and he felt it would continue even after she had wed.

After what felt like hours, they finally had all the decorations ready to be hung. Diana directed various servants on where she wanted the garlands to go. Elias noted that someone must have collected the yule log since it was decorated and waiting by the grand fireplace in the drawing room.

Once all the decorations were in place, except for the kissing balls, Diana sent the rest of the guests to rest and refresh themselves after the morning's exertions, but she'd asked Lydia and Elias to stay back with her.

After everyone had departed, aside from a single servant, Diana pointed toward the balls with mistletoe. "I shall leave you both to these."

Diana departed, and then a footman followed Elias and Lydia around while they pointed out the spots that they wanted the balls hung. When there was only one ball left, they found the most perfect secluded spot in a small alcove. "This shall be our secret hiding place," Elias said, dismissing the servant after they hung it in place.

"I find myself standing here beneath the kissing ball," he said, waving her to him. "You wouldn't wish to suffer any bad luck, would you?"

"You're a sneaky one," she said, grinning at him. But she hastened to him, close enough so he could pull her the rest of the way against him.

"I'm just resourceful, Beautiful," he said before placing several tender kisses on her lips. What he felt for her might not be love, but whatever it was, was quite strong. He didn't think he'd ever get enough of her, and he'd need to ensure that he made her his wife.

She pulled back to look at him. "We should both go freshen up. Your sister will surely want us all back down here soon."

Elias groaned. "I see you already have a good measure of Diana, because you are quite right."

He extended his arm to her. "I shall escort you upstairs."

Suddenly, he had that feeling again that they were being watched, but when he looked around, no one was there. Perhaps he was going mad. It was the only explanation.

⇒⟫⟩⟨⟪⇐

HALF AN HOUR later, there was a knock at Elias's chamber door. Part of him hoped it would be Lydia, but it would be far too scandalous for her to appear in his chamber in the middle of the day.

Not as scandalous as enjoying how his cock felt in her mouth, he reminded himself.

Pushing aside the memory before he would be forced to take himself in hand again, he opened the door. A footman held out a note. "The lady asked me to deliver this to you."

Elias took it and nodded, then closed the door. He unfolded

the missive and read it to himself.

Come now and meet me in our secret hiding place.

All attempts to get his cock to settle went by the wayside. Elias grinned to himself that Lydia had needed to see him again so soon. He supposed he couldn't wait to see her again as well, especially if the other guests hadn't returned downstairs quite yet.

Hurrying, he donned his coats again, not bothering to ring for Flint to assist. If he had his way, his appearance would be quite mussed from their little rendezvous.

Elias departed his chamber and hurried down to the small alcove where they had placed the last kissing ball. It was a darkened spot, but he could see a figure already there waiting for him. He approached.

"I sure am glad to see you, Beautiful," he said, pulling the figure to him.

"Elias," someone with a familiar voice said from behind him. Lydia.

He turned to see her standing there wide eyed, watching the scene unfold. He jerked his head back to the other figure, and the gaudy perfume consumed his senses. "What in the hell do you think you are doing?" he said to Lady Billings.

"Better that she knows the truth about us now, don't you think?" Lady Billings asked, running her hand down his chest and making his blood run cold. "It's not as if you would ever remain faithful to the little doe-eyed thing, even if you ever had some bacon-brained thought of marrying her."

Lydia hurried away.

"I'll deal with you later," Elias ground out at Lady Billings before taking off after Lydia. "Lydia, wait," he called after her. She had gotten a head start on him, but he caught up to her before she reached the stairs. He was thankful that while there were several servants who poked their heads out to see what the commotion was, there wasn't another guest in sight.

Elias grabbed her arm and pulled her into the closest room.

"That wasn't what it looked like," he blurted. He clasped both of her hands, but she pulled them away.

"Oh, so I didn't just hear you referring to the very woman you've been intimate with in the past with the same pet name you use for me? Even though you promised me that things were done between you."

He reached for her again, but she stepped back. "I thought it was you waiting for me."

She laughed. "And you expect me to believe that?" Lydia drew a deep breath and tears formed in the corners of her eyes. "So is 'Beautiful' what you call all the women? Is it easier than remembering our names? Or perhaps so you don't slip up and call us by the wrong name."

"Lydia, I swear to you. I have never referred to another woman in that way. And I believed it was you who was waiting for me. I only want you, and I intend to marry you. I just wished to speak with your father and mine first so I could declare my intentions."

"I don't doubt you intended to offer for me, my lord. But I require a faithful husband. I believe I am at least owed that measure of respect, and you have already proven that won't be you."

He reached forward and clasped her chin, holding it so he could stare into her eyes. She didn't move to get away from him, but the tears that had formed rolled down her cheeks and it made his heart sink into the pit of his stomach at how much pain the whole ordeal had caused her.

"I thought I was meeting you," he said slowly. "I would never be unfaithful to you. You must believe me. I want to marry you, have children with you, and live a contented, happy life together. That is all that I want. Please."

"So are you saying you love me?" she asked, her tone softening slightly but with a hesitant edge to it.

He drew a deep breath. Elias knew the matter would come up, but the timing was less than ideal, nor did he have a plan for how to broach the matter of love with her.

"I have a strong affection for you, and I care for you a great deal. But I cannot love you," he replied, and his heart immediately sank further as he watched her flinch as if he had slapped her.

Elias knew he'd messed up and chosen his words poorly. He wasn't prepared for the conversation and had bungled everything. "Allow me to explain."

"There is no need," she said, moving toward the door.

He hurried after her. "Please, Lydia."

"It's Miss Cary, my lord, and I need you to leave me be. I need to think, and I shall let you know if I wish to hear anything further from you."

"Please," he said again, fighting back a wave of emotion.

"Let me pass," she commanded, hardening to him so harshly that he wasn't certain she would ever allow him in her presence again.

He moved to the side and let her depart. Every fiber in his being wanted to force her to listen, to kiss her senseless and remind her that just because he couldn't say the words she wanted to hear didn't mean he didn't care more for her than anyone else in the entire world.

Elias went to the sideboard, thankful that it had been stocked with a decanter of brandy. He gave himself a healthy pour and downed it.

"Elias," Diana said, bursting into the room. "There you are."

"Here I am," he said, pouring himself another glass.

She eyed him curiously. "Papa needs us all right away."

"I'm in no mood." He would far rather continue to wallow in his misery and then think of some way to convince Lydia that they would have a wonderful life together, and he'd be the best husband she could ever ask for. Surely there was nothing his father could want that was more important than that.

"Well, that does not signify," Diana replied, appearing that her patience was fading. "Papa said it was urgent, and for me to fetch you now."

Hell and Damnation. Elias groaned in defeat. "Very well. We shall see what he is about."

He begrudgingly followed his sister to their father's study and saw that Jenny and Grace sat on the settee and his father sat across from them in a wing-backed chair. Diana closed the door behind them and then strode over to their sisters and sat on the settee with them, leaving Elias to take the empty chair near his father.

They all stared at their father, waiting for him to speak. Elias might have nudged his father along, but he was so lost in thought over Lydia, that he didn't much care at that moment.

Elias noticed that there was a bundle of packages on the table beside his father, then glanced at him and saw that his eyes were red as if he'd been crying.

"Father," Elias said softly.

The elder Lord Snowdon opened his mouth to speak and then closed it again.

"What is it, Father?" Elias asked, then glanced at Diana, who shrugged and then refocused her concerned gaze on their father.

"I...I had asked the servants to bring down some things of your mother's. I thought with Diana out in society now that she might like to have some of her mother's things if she should wed."

They sat in silence, waiting for what he would say next, allowing him a few moments to draw several breaths.

"And they found these among her things. When I had them packed up, I didn't go through anything, as I was far too devastated. But she had these gifts for each of us for Christmas that year. Before she..." His voice faltered at the last word, and Elias reached over and squeezed his father's arm.

Their father drew another long breath and glanced at each of his children, looking at Elias last. "I thought we should open them together in private, and I didn't wish to make you all wait until tomorrow."

The elder Lord Snowdon picked up each package and handed

it to its owner until they each held a parcel in their hands. Elias's chest heaved, already knowing that there would be a note and uncertain if he could handle reading the words of his mother just before she passed, but knowing that he had longed for the very thing from her for the last twelve years.

"Grace, you go first, sweetheart," their father said.

She gently tore at the packaging and then opened the box, pulling out a white blanket with hand stitched pink floral edging. Grace ran her fingers over the embroidery, knowing as the rest of them did that their mother had stitched it for her. She pulled out the note and read it to herself, crying harder at each word before she clutched the letter and blanket to her chest.

Jenny already had tears streaming down her cheeks when she opened hers. She pulled out a similar blanket, but with a different stitching, and done in blue. Elias recalled that from an early age, Jenny's favorite color had always been blue. After Jenny read her note, she buried her face in her hands, and Diana rubbed her back while fighting back her own sobs.

By the time Diana began opening hers, they were all overcome with emotion. Diana showed them a set of handkerchiefs that had been stitched with an elaborate floral design. And by the time Diana had finished reading her note, she had given up every effort to control her sobs and the three sisters were clutching each other on the settee.

Their father looked to Elias with ruddy cheeks and nodded, urging him to open his. Elias drew a deep breath and opened the package. It was also a set of handkerchiefs, but stitched with his initials and their family crest. He held them up to his face, tears forming in the corners of his eyes from the recognition of his mother's scent. The mix of lavender and vanilla that he hadn't smelled since that day before he left with his friends to the hunting cabin.

Taking a fortifying breath, he pulled the letter from his parcel and read it to himself.

Elias,

You are one of the five greatest loves of my life. I am beyond proud of the young man you are becoming and know that you are going to grow into one of the most respected lords of the peerage. As you continue to go off and learn the things that it takes to be a man in our society and fulfill your duties to the title, I hope you always remain my sweet, earnest boy with a heart full of love and laughter. Don't miss out on the other joys that make life worth living, as those are far greater than titles and money. If you need any proof of that, just look at our family and the love your papa and I have for you and your sisters.

Happy Christmas, my sweet boy,
Mama

Elias couldn't hold back the tears and emotion that he had choked down for far too many years, and allowed himself to weep. He always had to be the strong one. The one who eased everyone else's pain, and he hadn't realized how much he'd needed to hear from his mother. For her to call him her sweet boy. For her to tell him she's proud of him.

But would she still be proud of him if she could see the man he had become? Would she tell him he was a fool for running away from love with the only woman he had cared for? Truth was, he loved Lydia. He just couldn't bring himself to admit it. If his mother were alive, she'd have already told him fifty reasons why he was being a fool, and then she would push his hair back out of his face and call him her "sweet boy," and he'd take her advice as he always had. She had never steered him wrong.

Gaining control over his emotions, he glanced at his father, who had opened his package and was reading his letter. A pair of handkerchiefs sat on the arm of the chair and the paper shook in his hands as he read. Suddenly, he let out a small chuckle, and it shocked them all.

Once his father finished reading, he folded the letter and placed it in his breast coat pocket and rose from his seat. "Come here, my girls," he said. They all jumped up and ran to him, wrapping their arms around him where they could find a place.

He caught Elias's gaze and waved him over to join. Elias moved to join them, wrapping his arms around Jenny and Grace to join in the family hug.

"This was the best Christmas gift I think we could have received," their father said. "I hope you know how much I love you all."

There was a flurry of 'I love yous' all around the room and a few more hugs before they all released each other.

"What did Mama say to make you laugh, Papa?" Grace asked.

"That is something that is just for me and your mama," their father said, and Elias noticed a light blush reach his father's cheeks.

Elias could only assume what words might cause such a reaction. When he was a younger lad, it would have been quite gross to acknowledge the passion between his parents in that way, but as a grown man who was ready to take his own wife, he was glad that his parents had experienced an unwavering passion and desire for each other.

"We better rejoin our guests," Papa said.

Diana ushered her sisters out of the room, but Elias held back. "Father, might I speak with you?"

"Always, my boy," his father said. "Although I suppose you haven't been a boy for quite some time."

Elias gave him a soft smile. "I wish to ask for Lydia...I mean, Miss Cary's hand."

His father clasped his shoulder. "I had a feeling she would be the one for you, son. She is delightful. Are you marrying her merely because you find her attractive, or have you given over to the notion of marrying for love?"

"I love her, Father." Elias sighed, realizing that once he'd spoken the words aloud, he wasn't so afraid of doing so repeatedly.

"I'm so proud of you, son," his father said, pulling him into a tight hug. "You deserve to experience a life with true love. I look forward to calling Miss Cary a daughter."

Elias pulled back from his father with a deep frown etched on his face. "If she will accept me. I made a bit of a mess of things."

"Go to her, son. Tell her how you feel, and I am sure all will be well. And don't be too proud to grovel. I know from experience that women enjoy such things."

Elias would get down on his knees and beg at her feet if that was what it took. "I will speak to her now. Even if she is in her chamber. This cannot wait."

His father laughed. "I look forward to announcing the betrothal tonight at dinner."

Elias rolled his eyes at his father, but deep down, his heart danced with joy that his father was proud of his choice. He hurried out of the room and glanced around the drawing room to see if Lydia was among the guests who had congregated.

Checking a few other places, there was no sight of her, so he ran up the stairs and turned down the wing where her chamber was. He knocked lightly on the door and thought he heard movement on the other side of the door.

"Lydia," he said in a loud whisper. "It's me. Let me in, please."

There was a noise that sounded like a scuffle, and he tried the knob to find it locked.

"Lydia," he called again. "Please open the door."

Something that sounded like muffled cries reached his ears. Then he heard someone say, "Quiet."

Elias hurried to the door next to hers and ran his hand along the door frame, seeking one of the skeleton keys they kept nearby in case of emergencies. Once he had it in his hand, he rushed back to her door and let himself into the room.

When he saw the scene in the room, rage exploded from within him.

Durham had Lydia's arms pinned behind her back and a knife to her throat. He had tied a cravat around her head and into her mouth, holding her mouth open to gag her.

Durham smirked at him and tears streamed down Lydia's face as she focused her gaze on Elias. "Well, look who has shown up to interrupt our fun."

CHRISTINA DIANE

CHAPTER TWELVE
Lydia

LYDIA HAD TRIED to overpower Clint when he entered her chamber, but he had put the knife to her throat, and she'd known she had to bide her time until she could find the right opportunity to get away from him. She only hoped she could do so before he did unspeakable things to her. Given that he had already threatened her he would do so.

She had been so filled with anger and hurt from the conversation with Elias that she had been crying into her pillow and it allowed the man to catch her by surprise. He slipped the fabric around her head and into her mouth before she knew what was happening. When he turned her to face him once he gagged her, she saw the fury in his dark eyes.

"I'll make you mine, whether you like it or not," he had said as he pulled her arms behind her back and held them in place with one hand. "I have been biding my time to find a way to get to you, and imagine my good fortune when I found you were staying nearby."

As soon as she heard Elias outside her door, her heart raced faster. Partially from hope that his presence might give her the chance she needed to get away from Clint, and partially out of fear that the bastard would hurt Elias. As foolish as she was, she loved Elias. She had lost her heart to him forever, and she wouldn't be able to live knowing that her unfortunate past with Clint had resulted in any harm coming to him. This was her mess, not Elias's.

"Quiet," Clint had hissed in her ear when she struggled against the gag.

A few moments later, the door burst open, and Elias looked ready to go into a blind rage when Durham taunted him.

"Let her go, right fucking now!" Elias shouted at Clint.

"You may wish to close the door and lower your voice, or else I might have to do something drastic," Clint replied.

Lydia cried out against the gag when he pressed the knife harder into her neck.

Elias growled and closed the door, but Lydia noted he didn't lock it. He turned back to face where Clint held her hostage, his body shaking with anger.

"Durham, let her go now, and we can settle this between us men," Elias said through gritted teeth.

Clint laughed. "Unfortunately, I want nothing from you. But her, however," he paused and ran the back of the blade along the globes of her breasts, "she has many appealing assets."

Lydia focused her gaze on Elias, watching his entire body tense with his hands tightened into fists and his jaw set in a firm, clenched line.

"How did you get in here?" Elias asked.

The blackguard squeezed her wrists tighter. "It would seem Lady Billings is quite taken with you. I would be jealous seeing how she's had us both, but I think I shall walk away with the sweeter prize. The woman wasn't all that hard to manipulate once I told her of my 'undying love' for Lydia here, and how you would need the woman to soothe your broken heart, among other places, when I won Lydia."

Lydia recalled the note she received to meet Elias. She hadn't thought before that the missive appeared to be in a woman's hand. Elias had said that he thought it was Lydia who he was meeting. And why would he have sent Lydia a note if he intended to meet another woman? Lady Billings must have thought it would help push Lydia into Clint's arms.

"She's not going anywhere with you," Elias ground out, his stare boring into the man.

"You seem to think you have the upper hand here, Snowdon, and on that, you are mistaken."

Elias took a step forward and Clint moved as if he'd slice her throat, causing her to cry harder.

Holding his hands up, Elias stopped. "What do you want, Durham?"

"I want what was supposed to be mine. I saw you in the village getting far too cozy with my property and knew I had to claim her before you bedded her. I know from experience that she's quite willing."

She knew Clint wasn't the best of men, but she wouldn't have ever thought he could be as cold and diabolical as he was proving to be.

"How do you know I haven't?" Elias asked, staring the man down.

"Because I've had eyes on you. Good to know she has a filthy mouth on her. I'll be making good use of it."

Lydia wriggled against his hold, but he was too strong for her to break free. Fear radiated through her body at being forced to be with him. The only man she'd ever want was Elias. She would never again allow another man to touch her. Ever.

"You can't have her," Elias ground out. "She is my be-trothed."

Lydia's eyes went wide at the lie. Although once she got out of this, she would run right into his arms and tell him how much she loved him. Even if he couldn't say it back.

Clint laughed again, almost as if he'd come unhinged and was slipping further into madness. "That will make it all the sweeter when I have her virgin blood on my cock and my ring on her finger."

"I will kill you where you stand first," Elias seethed.

Lydia believed Elias would do so if the opportunity presented itself. Elias didn't have the air of a violent man, but she knew how fiercely he protected those that he cared about. He may not love her, but she knew he cared for her.

"If you come another step closer, I shall slice her throat before you do," he replied, as if it were of no consequence. "And you appear to be unarmed, so I think my chances are slightly better than yours. But feel free to assess the situation and decide for yourself."

Elias froze and glanced around the room, as if he were looking for something. Probably a weapon.

Several silent moments passed before Clint spoke again. "Perhaps your gentleman friend would like to watch while I take your maidenhead, my sweet. We could take care of matters right now." He shifted his attention to Elias. "And if you want to have at her after that, I'll let you. For a price, of course. I intend to sell her body to anyone willing to pay. That's what the lightskirt gets for thinking she can run away from me and send her bumbling papa to threaten me out of Town."

She watched as Elias drew a deep breath, his chest and shoulders heaving from anger. She knew he felt helpless, but she held onto hope that one of them would find a way out.

"How do you think you are going to get her out of here with no one stopping you?"

"The same way I'm keeping your pathetic, lovesick arse from coming near me. With this knife pressed against her throat."

"She'll run from you," Elias said, catching her gaze for a moment and then refocusing her attention on Clint.

She would never accept such a fate and allow herself to be at the horrid man's whim. She would run from him the first chance she got and never stop running.

"She won't," Durham said quickly. "Do you want to know how I know?" he asked, then glanced at Lydia, speaking to her. "Because I will murder your besotted fool and his entire family. Even those precious sisters of his." Clint smirked and then caught

Elias's hard stare again. "Although, I might keep Lady Diana around for a while. She could be useful. We'll see if she has the mouth of a strumpet on her too."

Lydia cried to herself as it appeared more likely that Clint might win. The man may be on the borderline of insanity, but he had found one of the few things that would keep her from running from him. She couldn't risk the lives of Elias and his family or subject Diana to the same torture she would face at his hands. She would have to go with him and comply if that is what it came down to.

The realization splintered her heart, and she fought the bile that rose in her throat. It would only make matters worse if she were to cast up her accounts while gagged. So she willed herself to remain calm. She would need her wits about her to find an opportunity to get out of his grip.

"In the spirit of the holiday and me being such a giving man, the choice is yours, Snowdon," Clint taunted. "Do you wish to step aside and let me remove her from here now, or do you wish to watch me unwrap my present and fuck her with a knife to her throat, and then I take her away?"

She saw tears form in the corners of Elias's eyes and his face was the darkest shade of red from how angry he was. He looked at her, regret in his eyes, and then looked back at Durham. She only hoped he knew that none of it was his fault.

Suddenly, a knock sounded on the door. It was her chance. It would be now or never.

"Enter!" Elias shouted, just as Lydia spun around so that she moved herself away from the knife. The way she turned bent Clint's arm back and forced him to release her hands.

Elias charged Clint as another man called, "What the bloody hell?"

"Hudson, help me!" Elias shouted at the man as he had Clint's hand with the knife pinned against the wall.

Lydia watched as Elias's friend, Lord Onslow, rushed over and pried the knife out of Clint's hand. As soon as he did, Elias began punching the man in the face repeatedly until the man fell into a pile on the floor.

"Elias," Onslow said, pulling him back. "That's enough."

Elias turned and instantly met her gaze, the rage fading from his expression as he rushed over to her. "Are you all right?" he asked, untying the cravat from around her face.

Lydia could only nod in response and threw herself into Elias's arms. He closed them tightly around her, placing tender kisses on her head. Elias pulled back and cupped her face with both of his hands, staring into her eyes as if he were on the brink of death and she was the salvation that he needed.

"What happened?" Lord Onslow asked.

"He was going to force her to marry him," Elias replied, his words thick with emotion, pulling her back against him and tightening his arms around her. "Among other things."

Onslow kicked Clint in the stomach in response, and Clint groaned. Served the bastard right.

"I need to get her away from him," Elias said to Onslow. "I don't want him breathing the same air as her. Help me tie him up and then we shall send for the magistrate."

Elias released her, only to help Onslow turn Clint onto his stomach. They used a bedsheet to tie his hands and feet together behind him so that he could not move his limbs even a single inch.

"Stay here and keep watch while I alert my father and send for the magistrate," Elias said to Onslow.

"He's not going anywhere," his friend replied, scowling at the pitiful excuse of a man who laid on the floor.

Elias turned back to her. "Come here, Beautiful," he said, sweeping Lydia into his arms to carry her from the room.

She wrapped her arms around his neck. "I'm sorry I stormed off earlier."

Elias stopped walking and stared at her. "Don't you dare apologize to me. I was the fool. Once I have you away from here and I know you are safe, I will tell you just what kind of fool I am."

Lydia laid her head against his chest and he resumed carrying her all the way downstairs and to a room that appeared to be a study. Perhaps his or his father's. He gently set her on the settee.

"Stay here." He didn't take his eyes off of her as he moved to grab the bellpull.

A few moments later, a footman entered. "Have my father and Lord Cary brought here straight away, but no one else. Tell them it is a matter of great import, but do not alarm any of the other guests."

The footman nodded and hurried off to do as Elias directed.

Elias returned and knelt before her.

"Before they arrive, I have something that I wish to say to you."

Lydia drew a breath, "I have something I wish to say to you too."

CHAPTER THIRTEEN

Elias

"I KNOW IT isn't the gentlemanly thing to do, but please allow me to speak first," Elias said. He needed to ensure she knew his words were true and were not influenced by anything that she might say to him.

She nodded and looked so beautiful for a woman who had just been in such a perilous situation. Her neck was red and there was a thin line where the knife had broken through her skin, causing a small amount of blood to escape. He wanted to go back upstairs and thrash the bastard again for each tiny drop of blood she lost because of Durham's horrid, disgusting behavior.

Elias pulled his handkerchief from his pocket and dabbed at the cut on her neck. Once he was certain she wasn't actively bleeding, he set the cloth aside and took her hands in his.

"I'm not a man of perfect words, nor am I typically a man of feelings," Elias started. "I pushed down and swallowed that part of myself after my mother died, believing that love held no place in my future and that I'd be all the better for it."

He drew a deep breath and watched as her eyes searched his. "But that changed when I met you, Beautiful. I fought it and told myself that what I felt for you wasn't love. But I was mistaken, as I am wholly and completely a besotted man." He paused and brought her hand to his lips to place a kiss on her knuckles.

"What I'm trying to say, Miss Lydia Cary, is that I love you. And I need to know before our fathers arrive if you wish to be my wife? Because I'm not certain that I can live without you."

For words that had been so hard for him to speak, and even harder for him to acknowledge, he found they rolled right off the tongue when his perfect woman sat before him. He knew it was true, that he loved Lydia with all of his heart. There would never be another woman for him, for as long as they were fortunate enough to have each other. Which would be for many decades to come if he had things his way.

Elias looked up at her and saw that tears had formed in the corners of her eyes. She grinned at him and then threw her arms around him. "I love you so much, Elias," she said into his neck.

"Does that mean you will marry me?" he asked, turning to kiss her brow.

She lifted herself so she faced him. "I want nothing more than to be your wife."

He leaned forward and pressed his lips against hers, needing her kiss more than he needed anything for the rest of his life, thankful that worse hadn't occurred that day, and that they had found their way to their rightful places at each other's sides. When she opened to him, he swept his tongue into her mouth, needing to taste her and brand her as his.

It would take a long time before the image of Durham holding her at knifepoint would no longer haunt him, but every kiss from her and every day spent with Lydia as his wife would help to erase it all. He could only imagine it was far worse for her, so he would do everything in his power to ensure she knew she would never fear for her safety and she would be deeply loved every day of their marriage.

"What is the meaning of this?" someone boomed from the doorway.

Elias broke their kiss, and realized they had been in quite the compromising position with him on his knees clutching onto Lydia, suckling her tongue. He glanced over to see his father and

Lord Cary staring at them.

Coming to stand, he held out his hand to Lydia and pulled her to join him. "Father, Lord Cary, we have a few important matters we must discuss."

"I'd say we do," Lord Cary said, glaring at Elias.

"Papa," Lydia warned, encouraging her father to keep his cool.

"Lydia was attacked," Elias said, watching as Lord Cary's expression shifted to one that was downright murderous. "It was Durham," Elias continued. "He had her a knifepoint, threatening to kidnap her in order to marry and rape her."

Lord Cary's face went white and Elias's father spoke first. "Where is he now?"

"Tied up in Lydia's chamber. Hudson is guarding him. We must send for the magistrate, but I wanted to inform both of you before I did so."

Elias's father reached for the bellpull as Lord Cary rushed to his daughter and threw his arms around her.

"Are you hurt, my sweet girl?" Lord Cary asked, pulling back from his embrace to look her over.

"No, Papa," she said. "Just a bit shaken."

Lord Cary turned his head to Elias. "Do I have you to thank for saving my daughter from the blackguard?"

Elias shook his head. "Not me. I stumbled upon the situation at the right time, but your daughter is quite capable. When the opportunity presented itself, she broke free and got herself away from Durham."

"He deserves a good thrashing," Lord Cary snarled.

"Well, I did give him that," Elias said sheepishly. "His face won't be recognizable for some time."

"Good man," Lord Cary said, extending his hand to Elias.

Elias took it and gave him a firm handshake.

A footman appeared, entering the study with them.

"I need you to have someone discreetly leave and fetch the magistrate. We need him here straight away, so have them escort him back directly," the elder Lord Snowdon said.

Before the man could depart, Elias caught his attention. "Send another footman to escort Lady Billings to us immediately."

The man hurried off and both of their fathers eyed him curiously.

"She was involved, and she will need to depart our estate. I won't have her sleeping under the same roof as Lydia or our family," Elias spat.

"I quite agree," his father said.

A few moments later, a footman entered, holding onto Lady Billings' elbow as they entered.

When she looked around and saw everyone scowling at her, she immediately turned on the tears.

"I did it for us, my love. Durham told me you and I would finally be together," she said to Elias. "He said that Miss Cary loved him, but was distracted by you. That if I helped him find a chance to speak with her, they would be married and you'd come back to me."

"Did he tell you he intended to hold me at knifepoint and threaten me with heinous things if I didn't marry him?" Lydia asked, stepping forward to face the woman.

Lady Billings shook her head. "No," she said, wide-eyed. "I had no idea. I would never have helped him if I had known that." The woman shifted her focus back to Elias. "You must believe me, Elias. I just wanted us to be together."

"I have already told you countless times over the last few years that we will never be together. And now you will leave my family's home and never speak to Lord Cary's family or a member of my family again."

"But Elias," she started.

"It's Lord Snowdon, my lady," Elias ground out, beyond done dealing with the woman. "I do not give you leave to address me informally and it is best that you remember it. And heed my warnings that you are not to address any of us again, nor mention anything that occurred here to another soul, or I shall ensure you receive the cut direct from every one of our acquaintances."

She bowed her head.

Elias's father spoke to the footman. "Escort Lady Billings to her chamber and remain with her while her maid packs her things, then ensure she is loaded into her carriage."

Lady Billings huffed, but followed along when the footman grabbed her arm to do as he was instructed.

"There is one more matter of import," Elias said to Lord Cary, while Elias's father grinned at his son knowingly.

"I'm in love with your daughter, my lord. I humbly request your permission to make her my wife. My father is here to attest to both of you," Elias said, catching Lydia's gaze, "that it was my intention to do so before this entire unfortunate series of events occurred."

He needed her to know that it wasn't the knife to her throat that sparked him to take action and name his feelings, but that he found himself outside of her chamber at that moment because he intended to ensure she knew how much he loved her.

"It's true," Elias's father said, mostly speaking to Lydia. "He declared his intentions to me earlier." His father grabbed Elias's hand and passed something to him.

Elias moved the small box through his fingers, eyeing his father curiously. He opened it and saw his mother's betrothal ring nestled in the box. Tears formed at the corners of Elias's eyes as he caught his father's gaze again.

His father beamed and gave him a small nod.

"If my daughter wishes to marry you, I have no objection to the match," Lord Cary said, having kept his focus fixed on Lydia.

"I do, Papa," Lydia said, clasping Elias's empty hand. "He's the man I love."

"Welcome to the family, my boy," Lord Cary said, patting Elias on the back.

Elias removed the ring from the box and took Lydia's left hand in his to slip it on her finger. "This was my mother's," he whispered.

Her eyes welled with tears as she glanced up at Elias and then she caught his father's gaze. "I am honored to wear her ring."

The elder Lord Snowdon stepped forward and scooped her into a hug. "I am honored to call you my daughter, dear girl." He pulled back and clasped her chin. "It just might be the best Christmas gift I've ever received. Now *you'll* have the tough job of keeping this son of mine in line."

Elias playfully nudged his father's shoulder. "Don't listen to him, Beautiful."

Lord Cary chuckled as he watched the scene unfold. "I believe we have a betrothal to announce this evening."

"That we do," Elias's father said proudly. "But first, let's ensure we rid the house of all the unwanted parties."

"Lead the way," Lord Cary said. Elias was certain that the man would throw a couple of punches of his own at Durham.

Both of their fathers departed the room to take over the handling of Durham and Lady Billings.

Lydia eyed the ring on her finger and then looked up at Elias with so much love shining in her eyes—it took Elias's breath away.

He pulled her to him and feathered several kisses along her jaw. "How soon can we wed, Beautiful?"

CHRISTMAS EVE HAD been a true joyous affair for the first time since Elias's mother had passed. His sisters had jumped up and down, practically screaming, when they learned that Lydia would become their sister. Lady Cary cried and hugged both of them so hard. It would appear that their two families would get on well together over the years.

Hudson wasn't all that surprised, given what he had walked in on. But Jude and Matt's jaws had both dropped when they made their announcement. But both had given Elias sincere hugs and welcomed Lydia into their group. Of all four of them, they all assumed Matt would be the first to take a wife, but fate had a plan of its own.

The four men stepped aside to have a drink together and toast to Elias's happiness.

"Who is going to join me for the fun of bachelorhood now?" Jude asked, slapping Elias on the back.

"You still have Matt and Hud," Elias said. "Surely you can drag one of them with you."

"It won't be the same," Jude said, giving him a momentary small frown. "But I'm happy for you."

"Thank you," Elias said. "Perhaps you gents might give love a chance?"

Hudson scoffed. "Who in the hell are you, and what did you do with my best friend?"

Elias shrugged. His friends wouldn't understand until they met the woman who would capture their heart and become the object of their every dream. "Your time will come."

Elias left them to their banter and returned to Lydia's side, who was chatting away with his sisters.

"I knew she would be our sister," Grace said as soon as Elias approached.

"How could you possibly know that, Grace?" Elias asked.

"She doesn't care if your cravat is mussed," she said in a matter-of-fact tone, as if it should have been obvious to all of them. "She had already told me so."

Elias and his sisters erupted into laughter.

"I am clearly missing something," Lydia said, obviously confused by the display.

Leaning close to her and brushing his lips against her ear, "I'll tell you later."

"Does that mean I shall see you tonight?" she whispered where only he could hear.

"If you think I'm sleeping apart from you, you are mistaken."

He caught her gaze and loved how her cheeks pinkened and

her eyelids had become heavy.

They had all decided that after Christmas, Elias would seek a special license so they could wed right away. If any gossip about the incident with Lady Billings were to get out, they would already be wed, which would help to manage the situation.

More importantly, Elias and Lydia wanted to wed quickly and begin their life together. Although he had every intention of anticipating their vows later that evening, and from the look of his betrothed, she would be agreeable to his intentions.

The guests gathered around the pianoforte and sang carols while Diana played. It had started to snow outside, which made the perfect backdrop to their joyous Christmas Eve. Elias glanced at each of his sisters, the joy radiating from their faces. He caught his father's gaze, and the elder Lord Snowdon was grinning from ear to ear.

Elias believed there would be many happy Christmases for their family in the years to come. Soon, perhaps even the next season, Diana would take a husband, and then children would join their family. They would have so many joyous things to celebrate, and Lydia would be at his side for every minute.

After the guests departed for their chambers, Elias pulled Lydia back to join him.

"I had your things moved to a chamber in the family wing," he said to her once everyone had left the room. "I don't want you to have to step foot in the other chamber ever again."

She wrapped her arms around his neck. "What a thoughtful husband you shall be."

"But you shan't be sleeping there, as I have plans to make quite merry with my betrothed this evening, if my lady is agreeable."

"We'll have to see how convincing you are," she said, smirking at him and pulling away.

He grabbed her wrists and pulled her back against him. "Do you prefer my wicked words or my wicked touch, Beautiful?"

"Why choose? When I know you shall give me both," she

said, pushing away from him, glancing over her shoulder as she walked toward the doorway.

Elias hurried after her and swept her into his arms, loving the stream of giggles she released when he did so.

"Take me to your bed," she said against his ear.

"Our bed," he corrected, carrying her to the staircase. He hurried up the stairs and swept into his chamber, kicking the door closed behind them.

He set her on the bed and removed the slippers from her feet, then kicked off his boots. Standing before her, he caught her gaze as he unbuttoned his coats and shrugged out of them, letting them fall to the floor.

"You're unwrapping my present for me," she whined.

He laughed. "Please accept my apologies, Beautiful." Elias held his arms out to his sides. "You can unwrap yours first, and then I'm unwrapping mine."

Lydia came up on her knees on the bed, and his cock throbbed hard against his breeches. She pressed her lips to his as she pulled his shirt free from his breeches and then unfastened each button with agonizing slowness.

She ran her hands along his chest as she pushed the fabric over his shoulders and then down his arms until it joined his other clothing on the floor. He drew a breath when she kissed his chest. "You are even more delightful without your clothes on," she said between kisses.

"I am pleased you think so, my lady. I haven't even done anything yet."

She worked the buttons of his breeches, and then pushed them down his hips. Elias stepped out of them as fast as he could and then removed his socks.

When he caught her gaze, she licked her lips and sent a jolt straight to his cock.

"My turn," he growled.

He pulled her against him, taking her lips in a searing kiss as he unfastened the buttons behind her without looking at them.

Once he had unfastened enough to loosen her dress, he lifted it over her head and tossed it away.

His lips found hers again as he untied her stays and then pulled them over her body with her chemise. She was completely naked before him, except for her long stockings.

Picking her up at the waist, she wrapped her legs around him and sucked where his neck and shoulder met like the temptress his future wife had proven to be. He pulled each of the pins out of her hair, dropping them on the floor until her hair fell down around her.

Elias ran his fingers through her long, soft locks, breathing in the intoxicating scent of lilies.

"Make me yours, Elias," she whispered in his ear.

"You are already mine, Beautiful." And she always would be.

She sucked the lobe of his ear into her mouth and then gave it a light bite before she brushed her lips against his ear again. "In every way," she whispered. "I want you inside of me."

Elias pulled the coverlet back and then turned, with her still wrapped around him, and sat on the bed. "We're going to make sure you are good and ready for me."

He scooted them back further on the bed, and then untangled her legs from around him and laid back flat on the bed.

"What are you doing?" she asked.

"Getting in position for you. You're going to straddle my face."

She looked every bit the goddess, sitting on top of him, her breasts bobbing with her tightly budded nipples, and confusion marring her face.

Unable to resist, he sat back up and sucked one bud into his mouth, making her moan and squirm with her bare arse rubbing against his cock. He picked up his head. "Come here," he said before laying back down.

"I'll hurt you," she said.

"You won't. I assure you."

He pulled her to shift her position, so that she had placed a knee on each side of his head. Her core hovered over him just where he could reach, running his tongue along the seam.

"Elias," she moaned.

"I'm going to make you come, and you move and ride my face however you wish."

She whimpered and moaned from his words, but her body responded by widening her knees, sinking her lower so her slit was in a perfect position. He found her nub first and then sucked and licked. Lydia immediately started moving against him, and he smiled against her wet heat. He wanted her to be his confident, beautiful temptress.

Elias sheathed two fingers inside of her and worked them hard, teasing the places he knew would bring her the most pleasure.

Lydia responded by rocking her hips, taking what she wanted from him.

"That's it, Beautiful," he encouraged, "ride my face until you come, and then I'll show you just how hard you're making my cock."

He didn't think his cock could get any harder. The thought of burying himself inside of her was enough to undo him. He licked and sucked her pearl while he increased the speed with his fingers, which made her move herself harder against him.

She released a steady stream of moans and her breathing came in ragged pants until she stilled and he felt her core tighten and pulse around his fingers. He removed his fingers and replaced them with his tongue, needing to taste the proof of her climax.

When she slumped, he reached for her, picking her up and laying her on the bed so that he could shift to hover over her.

"Are you certain you wish to do this before we are married?" he asked her as she settled in beneath him, her long, dark hair splayed out to the side.

"More than anything," she sighed.

He would have respected her wishes had she wanted to wait, but he needed to be inside her. To join with her and for them both to know they belonged to each other forever. Elias positioned himself at her opening. "I will do my best not to hurt you, but it should only be this first time."

She nodded and captured his gaze. "I trust you."

Elias took her lips in a tender kiss. After all that had occurred, he hadn't realized how much he needed to hear those words from her. He pushed the head of his cock inside of her, and pushed only an inch at a time, allowing her to adjust to him. He'd never been with a virgin before, and he hoped he was going slow and careful enough.

When he was almost there, he pushed the rest of the way in and she shifted beneath him.

"I'm sorry, Beautiful. It should feel better soon." He hated that he had to hurt her, as he would happily bear any of her pain.

He nibbled at her bottom lip, then sucked her tongue into his mouth, distracting her while she adjusted to him. She ran her hands along his back and he slowly moved within her, teasing her with his length.

"Oh, yes, Elias," she moaned. "Do that."

"Anything you wish, you shall always have."

He withdrew and then entered her again, and he was rewarded with a stream of unintelligible words, and he thought perhaps a couple of profanities too.

"Wrap your legs around me," he commanded gently, then gave her another long kiss.

She did as he said, and he thrust into her again. Nothing had ever felt better or more right than being inside of her. Joining with her in a way that was primal and just for them, forever. She would always be his home.

Elias increased his speed, and she arched her back and panted. His temptress begged him with her body for him to give her more. She moved with him, meeting his thrusts, taking an active role in their lovemaking. Oh, the wicked things he'd teach her.

"That feels so good," she said between pants. She ran her hands along his body and his skin heated beneath her touch.

"You are so tight and perfect, Beautiful. I shall never get enough of you." Truer words had never been spoken.

He shifted one of his hands down to her hip and lifted it slightly so he could enter her deeper.

"Yes," she cried out when he thrust again. "God, yes."

"I love you," Elias said, slowing his movements so that he rocked into her with tender movements.

She looked at him and cupped his cheek. "I love you so much."

He increased his speed again, ready to bring her to the edge and watch as she shattered and soared and everything between. She released a few more unintelligible words, and her eyes squeezed shut.

"Eyes on me, Beautiful," he commanded. He couldn't miss witnessing how they gave each other everything they had. All the affection, all the pleasure, and most importantly, all the love between them.

Lydia opened her eyes, which met his. Elias increased his speed, pulling out and thrusting into her as deep as he could.

"Don't take your eyes off of mine while I make you come on my cock."

In two more thrusts, she clenched around him and it undid him. The pulsing of her core milked the seed from his cock as he buried himself deep inside of her. Their eyes never left each other. He'd never spent inside of a woman, and nothing had ever been more perfect or more right than the two of them in that moment.

"That was...that was..." she started, her chest rising and falling where she tried to catch her breath. "I had no idea."

"I didn't either," he said honestly. "It's never been like that."

The moment was charged and consuming, and love radiated through every fiber of his being for the woman beneath him. He would have only lived less than half a life if he had missed out on loving her, and he finally understood what his father meant.

As much as he didn't want to move from his place on top of

her, Elias climbed from the bed and went to the wash basin.

"Where are you going?"

He returned with a cloth and used it to clean between her legs. "There is blood your first time, so I am just cleaning you."

After he finished wiping between her legs, he used the cloth on himself. He went and placed it back by the wash basin, and then locked his chamber door. Laughing to himself that he should have already done so.

Finally, he climbed back into the bed, both of them lying beside each other with his head on a pillow and hers on his chest. They fit together perfectly.

He pulled the covers over them and brushed her hair back out of her face, then held her tight against him.

The moon was bright and he could see the snow still falling outside the window.

"Happy Christmas, Beautiful."

EPILOGUE

Elias

Christmas Eve 1812

ELIAS HAD BEEN eager for weeks for him and Lydia to celebrate their first official Christmas together as husband and wife. The day after Christmas, a year ago, he went to Town and procured the special license and then they were wed the following day with their family and friends in attendance. Hudson and Diana served as their witnesses, and the family had a joyous wedding breakfast before Elias and Lydia left their guests to celebrate without them, and didn't show their faces for over a week.

He watched as his father walked around the drawing room with Elias and Lydia's daughter, pride and love radiating from the elder Snowdon as he gazed upon his first grandchild. He had broken down in sobs when he learned they had named her Emily, after Elias's mother.

"I think she just smiled at her grandpapa," he called Elias. "You did, didn't you, my sweet girl," he cooed at the babe.

Jude walked over and looked at the babe and then at Elias's father. "I believe she did. And thank goodness she took after her mother." Jude caught Elias's gaze and smirked.

"I quite agree," Elias replied, waving him off. "Although she has my eyes." The sapphire blue eyes his family was known for had passed to another generation.

Jude, Hudson, and Matt were all still unwed. Jude and Hudson had gathered at the Snowdon estate for the holidays. Diana was too far along in her pregnancy to travel, so they would all go to spend a few days with her, closer to when the babe would come.

Hannah had gone to spend the holidays with Diana and her husband, who Matt had become close friends with. So he had decided to spend the holidays there too. Hudson had tried to stop Hannah from going since Matt would be there, since another year had passed with no resolution between them, nor did anyone know why Hudson couldn't let matters go. But Diana wrote to Hudson and gave him a written set down for trying to keep her friend from her while she was in a delicate condition. He grumbled like he usually did about such things, but ultimately allowed Hannah to go.

It was a smaller group that year for the holiday with just the group of men, his father and sisters, and Lydia's parents in residence, as well as little Emily, and Elias preferred it that way. No longer did they need to fill the house with chaos to avoid the sadness of losing their mother, as they had so much love to be thankful for. He had decided the day he married Lydia that, from then on, he would make the most of every moment with his family.

Lydia strolled into the room, and his breath caught. She still had that hold over him, and he'd never tire of the way she laughed, or the way she sang to their daughter, or the way her eyes darkened when he drove her over the cliff of unbridled ecstasy.

She came over to him and sat on the arm of his chair. "Our sisters are almost ready to go cut the greenery. I have asked Jude and Hudson to assist each of them." Lydia leaned closer and brushed her lips against his. "And the cabin is ready for us."

His cock twitched, knowing what awaited him when they snuck out to have a repeat of their first Christmas Eve. "Have I told you how much I love you, Beautiful?"

"Perhaps not in the last couple of hours," she teased, placing a kiss on his temple. "Are you almost finished?" she asked, pointing toward the parchment in his lap.

"Yes, I was going to fold it now."

Lydia kissed his temple again and rose from the armrest. "Well, do so and don your greatcoat, then we shall all depart."

Elias looked down at the parchment. He had decided he would honor his mother's tradition of writing letters on Christmas. He had already written Lydia's, and included a couple of passages that were sure to make her blush and lead to a more than pleasant, mutually beneficial Christmas night.

But he had been working to get the one for Emily just right. She wouldn't be able to read it for herself until she was older, but he would read it to her on Christmas Day and then save it for her when she was older. Elias held up the parchment and read it again to himself.

Sweet Emily,

Every time I look at you, I see the best parts of your mama and me, and I couldn't love you more. I would give you the moon if you asked for it, and I hope that you always know how loved you are. You have the love of so many people in your life, and love is never something to take for granted or fear. There is nothing more important than the people we love, and your mama and I are going to make sure you grow up knowing that you shall never settle for anything less than what you deserve.

We haven't told anyone else yet, but your mama is going to give you a brother or sister several months from now. So take it easy on her, since she's trying to hide how sick she feels.

I love you, sweet girl,
Papa

Elias glanced up at the candle burning on the mantle for their mother, thinking about how she would've been the best of grandmamas. He could only hope that she might smile down on them from wherever her spirit was, that she had found peace in knowing that they had all turned out all right.

He stood to join the family outside, and turned back to look at the candle again, closing his eyes for a moment, hoping his mother might hear the words spoken from his heart.

Happy Christmas, Mama.

About the Author

Christina Diane enjoys weaving stories of love and passion set in the Regency era from her home in Northern Maine. She usually has her kindle in hand (reading a Regency romance, dark romance, or thriller) when she is not writing or chasing after her family! Along with her husband and two boys, her family includes their three French bulldogs who go everywhere with them. The entire family is always up for their next adventure. Aside from her family, writing, and books, she loves Bridgerton, the Grinch, Jessica Rabbit, horror movies, cold brew, yoga, Hamilton, and speaking in obscure quotes from movies and TV shows. Christina loves chatting with her readers and talking about great reads, so please contact her on socials!

Website: christinadianebooks.com
Facebook: christinadiane
Instagram: christinadianeauthor
TikTok: @christinadianeauthor
Twitter: @CDianeAuthor
YouTube: @ChristinaDianeAuthor
Pinterest: christinadianebooks
Bookbub: bookbub.com/authors/christina-diane
Goodreads:
goodreads.com/author/show/50735966.Christina_Diane
Amazon: amazon.com/stores/Christina-Diane/author/B0D7Z15DQD
Readers Group: facebook.com/groups/christinadiane